AF440093

THE TREBLE WITH MURDER

SCHOOL OF HARD ROCKS MYSTERIES

CHRISTY BARRITT

Copyright © 2021 by Christy Barritt

All rights reserved.

No part of this book may be reproduced in any form or by any electronic or mechanical means, including information storage and retrieval systems, without written permission from the author, except for the use of brief quotations in a book review.

COMPLETE BOOK LIST

Squeaky Clean Mysteries:

    #1 Hazardous Duty

    #2 Suspicious Minds

    #2.5 It Came Upon a Midnight Crime (novella)

    #3 Organized Grime

    #4 Dirty Deeds

    #5 The Scum of All Fears

    #6 To Love, Honor and Perish

    #7 Mucky Streak

    #8 Foul Play

    #9 Broom & Gloom

    #10 Dust and Obey

    #11 Thrill Squeaker

    #11.5 Swept Away (novella)

    #12 Cunning Attractions

#13 Cold Case: Clean Getaway

#14 Cold Case: Clean Sweep

#15 Cold Case: Clean Break

#16 Cleans to an End

While You Were Sweeping, A Riley Thomas Spinoff

The Sierra Files:

#1 Pounced

#2 Hunted

#3 Pranced

#4 Rattled

The Gabby St. Claire Diaries (a Tween Mystery series):

The Curtain Call Caper

The Disappearing Dog Dilemma

The Bungled Bike Burglaries

The Worst Detective Ever

#1 Ready to Fumble

#2 Reign of Error

#3 Safety in Blunders

#4 Join the Flub

#5 Blooper Freak

#6 Flaw Abiding Citizen

#7 Gaffe Out Loud

#8 Joke and Dagger

#9 Wreck the Halls

#10 Glitch and Famous

Raven Remington

Relentless 1

Relentless 2 (coming soon)

Holly Anna Paladin Mysteries:

#1 Random Acts of Murder

#2 Random Acts of Deceit

#2.5 Random Acts of Scrooge

#3 Random Acts of Malice

#4 Random Acts of Greed

#5 Random Acts of Fraud

#6 Random Acts of Outrage

#7 Random Acts of Iniquity

Lantern Beach Mysteries

#1 Hidden Currents

#2 Flood Watch

#3 Storm Surge

#4 Dangerous Waters

#5 Perilous Riptide

#6 Deadly Undertow

Cape Corral Keeper

Seagrass Secrets

Driftwood Danger

Beach House Mysteries

The Cottage on Ghost Lane

Carolina Moon Series

Home Before Dark

Gone By Dark

Wait Until Dark

Light the Dark

Taken By Dark

Suburban Sleuth Mysteries:

Death of the Couch Potato's Wife

Fog Lake Suspense:

Edge of Peril

Margin of Error

Brink of Danger

Line of Duty

Cape Thomas Series:

Dubiosity

Disillusioned

Distorted

Standalone Romantic Mystery:
The Good Girl

Suspense:
Imperfect
The Wrecking

Sweet Christmas Novella:
Home to Chestnut Grove

Standalone Romantic-Suspense:
Keeping Guard
The Last Target
Race Against Time
Ricochet
Key Witness
Lifeline
High-Stakes Holiday Reunion
Desperate Measures
Hidden Agenda
Mountain Hideaway
Dark Harbor
Shadow of Suspicion
The Baby Assignment

The Cradle Conspiracy

Trained to Defend

Mountain Survival

Nonfiction:

Characters in the Kitchen

Changed: True Stories of Finding God through Christian Music (out of print)

The Novel in Me: The Beginner's Guide to Writing and Publishing a Novel (out of print)

____

CHAPTER ONE

YEARS OF THERAPY have helped me to realize that everyone has issues. Some of us just hide ours better than others.

Nothing reminded me of that fact more than revisiting my past.

Which was precisely what I was doing right now.

I stared at the majestic stage in front of me—the one draped with a burgundy velvet curtain and covered with a rich mahogany floor—before closing my eyes.

People around me chatted as a sound check took place for an upcoming talent competition. A young woman, probably twenty, stood at the microphone singing a tune from the musical *Les Mis*.

Her voice was nice, but, as she tried to hit a high

note, her pitch reached for the heavens only to fizzle in the stratosphere.

I tried not to cringe.

I had to make it a conscious habit to turn off from audio-sensory compulsions. For some people, noises were just noises. For me, every little sound formed a symphony—or a train wreck—in my mind. My pitch perfect abilities, combined with hyperacusis and a complex echoic memory, made me a G sharp in a sea of flats.

I opened my eyes again and stared at the majestic auditorium around me. I couldn't believe I was here at the Grand Isle Music Conservatory again after all these years.

My hands gripped the railing as I stood at the back of the room and gave myself a mental pep talk. *You can do this, Camryn.*

Footsteps sounded beside me. The heaviness of the steps indicated a man. The sound of slick leather on the carpet indicated dress shoes. The whisk of fabric—probably silk infused—indicated dress pants.

I opened my eyes and turned toward the brisk noise.

"If it isn't Camryn Paine." Dr. Joseph Hannon's deep voice rang out as he paused beside me.

I glanced up at his familiar face. Aging hadn't been kind to my friend. The hair atop his head was almost completely gone. His jowls hung loose and accentuated his round face. Dark circles under his eyes made him look tired.

I leaned forward as he offered a kiss on the cheek. "Joseph. It's good to see you."

Joseph was chancellor of the college, which was located outside of Savannah, Georgia. His grandfather had started the music conservatory more than one hundred years ago. Sebastian Hannon was now known as one of the greatest musical composers of the last century. His work had been featured in concerts all over the world.

Joseph and I had attended school here together another lifetime ago.

"We're so thrilled you're going to be joining us." Joseph practically beamed as he stared at me before the brightness suddenly left his gaze. "Especially in light of everything that's happened lately."

I frowned. I'd be taking over as Chief Communications Officer at the conservatory. A string of unfortunate events had occurred at the college—including an administrator who'd embezzled money and a student named Velvet Matthews who'd fallen, hit her head on the edge of a bathtub, and died.

I'd been brought in on a temporary basis to do damage control. That's what I did.

I slayed dragons. Dragons that ruined reputations, that caused lost funding, that tarnished images.

I found issues and dealt with them. Though my title was officially public relations my skills went far beyond that. I'd learned that to deal with crises, you had to get to the root of the matter.

For that reason, I not only handled the media, but I used the skills I'd learned to dig deeper. During my last job, at a pharma company, I'd managed to find the corporate spy who was selling top secret information to a competitor. When the information went public, the company who hired me looked heroic and the other . . . well, its stocks had plummeted.

Some people called me a fixer.

Too bad I couldn't fix my own life.

I glanced at the stage again and saw someone swagger into the spotlight toward the student at the microphone—a student who now rubbed her eyes as if she wanted to cry.

My breath caught when the new figure came into view. Was that . . . ?

"Yes, that's Weston Turner." Joseph seemed to

read my thoughts as he followed my gaze. "I wasn't sure if you were aware he worked here now."

My hands went back to the brass railing, and I gripped it until my knuckles turned white, until I heard the rub of damp skin against metal as sweat dotted my palms. "I wasn't."

"He started two years ago. It looks like the Dynamic Duo is back."

Dread pooled in my stomach. That's what people used to call Weston and me. We'd been inseparable—on and offstage.

"He's a favorite among students," Joseph continued.

"I bet." Weston had always been everyone's favorite—including mine.

That part of my life seemed like so long ago now. I thought I'd left that heartbreak behind. And I had.

So much had happened since then. I'd married Phil. Abandoned my musical career. Scarlett had been born, and Phil and I had raised our daughter together.

Then Phil had died, and Scarlett had gone off to college.

Empty nest had set in for me at the ripe age of forty-three.

Now I was here.

I was starting over again in a new place—except it wasn't that new. This music conservatory held more memories than my mind could contain.

I sucked in a deep breath and tried to focus my thoughts.

As I did, more noises crackled around me.

The AC blared from an overhead vent, a small clank inside it as if something were loose.

Joseph tapped a shoe on the carpet, the rhythm steady and matching the music.

The student continued warming up onstage, her nerves causing pitch problems. A woman—probably a voice instructor—whispered something to her, no doubt correcting her.

Wheels rolled unseen at the back of the stage as the crew worked on the set.

Each sound made up a small part of life around me. The noises painted pictures that weren't always seen with the eye but composed part of our vibrant existence.

Joseph still stared at me, a friendly look in his gaze. "When did you arrive in town?"

I tucked a blonde hair behind my ear. "A few hours ago. I dropped off my suitcases—and a few other things—at my apartment and then headed here. I partly wanted to stretch my legs and partly wanted to get a feel for this place again, to get my bearings. I know there's still an hour before I'm supposed to meet with you."

"Do you ever not have your bearings?" He raised an eyebrow at me, giving me a knowing look.

I decided not to bore him with the details of my life—not to mention the hours of therapy I'd already gone through to try to cope with the trauma that haunted me. I found no shame in admitting that I'd been meeting with a counselor for years now.

For me, therapy was like eating. It was a necessity. Those sessions helped me process life.

It seemed like such a shame to be able to fix every crisis around me but not be able to fix myself.

I remembered Joseph's question. *Do you ever not have your bearings?*

"You might be surprised." I offered a quick smile.

"Well, you look fabulous. In fact, I'm not sure you've aged since I saw you last."

"I'm sure you say that to everybody."

Joseph, a former opera singer, was uptight and had a deep voice that I could listen to for hours. Kind but nervous, he used to sweat so much his clothes would be drenched.

His smile faded. "I mean it when I say we're glad

to have you here, Camryn. I have a lot I need to update you on."

"I look forward to getting busy." I pulled out my phone. "Speaking of which, I promised Scarlett that I'd send her a video when I got here. She wants to see what my old alma mater is like."

I pulled up the camera and scanned the massive auditorium so my daughter could get a feel for the size of this place.

It was a big deal to be here. A really big deal.

As I turned back to the stage, I saw the student at the microphone was still fighting tears. The poor thing just couldn't seem to move past her stage fright.

Joseph followed my gaze. "As I'm sure you know, it's Harvest Week here at the school. Just as we've done for decades, our festivities begin with cookouts and pumpkin carving and end with the Trills and Thrills Ball as well as our annual talent competition this weekend."

I glanced around and noticed there weren't any students sitting in the seats waiting for their turn. "Where are the other contestants?"

Joseph frowned. "We had an issue with sabotage a few years back, so now only one contestant at a time is allowed inside."

"Sabotage? Really?"

"We have a guest judge every year who's very . . . what's the word? Appealing. Someone who's a star-maker. Who could easily get someone's foot in the door of a record label. It's made the event very competitive."

"I can imagine."

He nodded toward the girl at the microphone. "That's Heather Klein. Her mom is Rebecca Haggard. Now Rebecca Klein."

My eyes widened. "My old roommate, Rebecca Haggard?"

"She's the one."

"Wow . . . what a small world." Now that Joseph mentioned it, I could see the resemblance. Heather had her mom's high cheek bones and thick, golden hair.

"Isn't it, though? We pride ourselves in having several generations of families accepted into our program."

I stared at Heather. In some ways, she reminded me of my Scarlett with her blonde hair and slim build. I'd really thought Scarlett might come here and follow in my footsteps. Another part of me was glad she'd gone the opposite route.

As I continued to watch Heather, I heard a gasp. A gurgle. A grunt.

I sucked in a breath as I tried to process what was happening.

Then Heather collapsed.

Her instructor rushed toward her.

My heart pounded in my ears.

What had just happened?

Before the question could leave my lips, Joseph had the phone to his ear. 911? Probably.

I knew we didn't have time to waste.

I darted toward the stage, desperate to see what had happened . . . and to figure out how I might be able to fix this situation.

CHAPTER TWO

AN HOUR LATER, I stood near the front of the stage and tried to comprehend this tragic turn of events. Everyone had assumed Heather passed out from nerves.

But when we'd reached the stage, she didn't have a pulse.

Paramedics had arrived five minutes later, and Heather was already gone, despite all the efforts to revive her. However, looking at Heather, nothing indicated what had happened to her. No wounds or hemorrhages or anything else offered a clue as to what might have caused her death.

What had happened to her? A heart attack? An aneurysm?

What could cause someone her age to die so suddenly, so quickly?

And what about those sounds I'd heard just before she'd collapsed? The gurgling? The grunt?

Unrest jostled inside me.

Nothing was normal about a student dropping dead on the stage.

The police had arrived and sequestered everyone who'd been in the Hannon Auditorium until law enforcement could collect each person's name and contact information.

Everyone appeared to be in shock as they stood around with blank expressions, arms crossed over their chests, and murmured words being exchanged.

Meanwhile, Heather lay on the stage, a sheet draped over her as the medical examiner knelt beside her.

"This is so horrible," a woman a few feet away whispered to the man beside her.

I observed her a moment. She was a plump woman in her early fifties with bobbed brown hair. She wore rumpled khakis and a stained white top. The man she talked to wore coveralls with the name "Harvey" stitched across the front.

Maintenance and housekeeping? It seemed like a good guess.

"It really is horrible," the man said. "First Velvet and now ..."

"It almost seems like this place is cursed or something."

Their words caused a knot to form in my throat.

I stepped closer to them. "Did either of you see or hear anything out of the ordinary?"

They glanced at each other before shaking their heads.

"No, I can't say I did," the woman said. "I was cleaning the floors in the lobby when I heard the commotion."

"And I was changing a lightbulb in the men's restroom." Harvey shrugged. "Sorry."

The woman's eyes brightened as she looked at me. "Aren't you ... Camryn Paine? The woman who sang 'I've Got Everything If I've Got You'?"

"That's me. I'm sorry to meet under these circumstances."

"I'm Anita." She let out a breath. "I'm so honored to meet you."

I politely thanked her, not really wanting to dive into this conversation right now—not when so much tragedy hung around us. I'd rather keep the focus on Heather.

"My daughter always sang that song when she did the county fair circuit," Anita continued.

I kept my eyes mostly on the stage, only glancing at Anita on occasion to be polite. "I'm honored. Is your daughter a student here?"

"No, she decided she wanted to be a teacher instead. Anyway, it's so nice to meet you."

As they walked away, I frowned and shifted, careful not to nudge the video camera set up beside me. It wasn't unusual to record these rehearsals so students could evaluate themselves. Self-assessment was important.

I turned my attention back to the scene in front of me and tried to tune in to the various conversations taking place in the room. If I concentrated, I could separate one from the other. It was a talent that came with my neuroses.

"Do you think Heather ate peanuts?" someone whispered.

"She's too smart to do that."

"Maybe it was an accident."

"I suppose it *could* have been. But she was usually so careful."

I stored those facts away. Had she died from a peanut allergy? That would fit the sounds I'd heard.

But I wasn't convinced.

Call me crazy, but I'd picked up on a few things in the course of my life. Until his death, my husband had run a successful private security firm. The reins had then been handed over to Joel, my brother, a former cop.

That wasn't to mention the fact that my father had been a career criminal. Basically, I felt like I knew crime inside and out because of my experiences.

Another conversation across the room caught my ear.

"This show is doomed," a college boy said.

"I know, right? First, Jana got food poisoning. Then Jordan broke his leg, and Beck was in the car accident. Now Heather . . ."

I absorbed their words, my intuition still screaming that there was more to this. There *had* to be.

I wasn't officially on the job yet, but I knew I was going to have to accelerate my start date. I didn't care as much about the public relations aspect of Heather's death as I did about the grief that hung in the air.

I remained near the front row—on the fringe of the action—watching everything going on.

This was my process until it was time to jump

into action. Then I'd take center stage, do my job, and then retreat again.

That dichotomy confused some people, but I'd learned that this was who I was—introverted by nature but extroverted by profession. I couldn't try to be anybody else, even if the me God had created was a confusing mess at times.

My gaze fluttered across the stage again until stopping on Weston Turner.

I hadn't seen him in person for years.

He still looked like the Weston I knew, with his brown hair with reddish highlights. He had a barely there beard and mustache now, and his build had filled out. His eyes sparkled with charisma. His jeans and plaid shirt almost made him look like a cowboy, even though he'd grown up in the suburbs.

I'd been there when he'd ridden a horse the first time, and it hadn't been pretty.

I hid a smile as the memory played in my mind.

He still had swagger in his steps and a killer smile that gave women something to daydream about.

As expected, right now Weston was in the thick of things. He talked to students. Rested his hand on their shoulders in comfort. Murmured reassuring words to them.

He'd always been such a people person, and others were drawn to him. The opposite of me, really. Sure, I'd learned those skills, but they didn't come naturally to me like they did to Weston.

I continued watching, listening.

As I did, everything went dark around me.

Several people gasped. One person let out a cry. Footsteps shuffled.

Darkness plunged deep in the windowless room.

I braced myself as I waited for the lights to come back up. For someone to turn on a flashlight.

For something.

Instead, everything felt suspended.

The next instant, I heard footsteps—moving quickly.

Then two hands shoved me, and I tumbled to the floor.

A FEW SECONDS LATER, lights flooded the room again.

I cringed as I sat up, and an ache shot through my hip.

Falls didn't seem as funny in my forties as they had when I was younger—this one even more so since I was pushed and my hip had hit a wooden armrest.

I heard more footsteps, as if someone else was running. A moment later, Weston strode down the center aisle, his muscles bristled.

He must have felt someone run past and chased after him.

Clearly, he hadn't caught him.

Instead, Weston paused in front of me, put his

hand on my elbow, and helped me to my feet. "Camryn . . . are you okay?"

I nodded, still feeling dazed from the surprise encounter. "I think so."

As he continued to grip my elbow, I felt a shock of electricity—one that unnerved me. I stepped away and quickly smoothed my pencil skirt in a last-ditch effort to look composed.

But as my gaze caught with Weston's, years of unspoken conversations drifted between us. We'd gone from being everything to each other to being nothing. The memories caused my throat to tighten.

"Let me get a paramedic to check you out." A deep voice pulled me from my battered thoughts.

I glanced at the sound and saw Detective Garrison standing near. He'd introduced himself to everyone when he arrived, and, right now, I was thankful for the interruption.

The man was probably thirty years old, with thick dark hair and a quiet demeanor. He had a square face and kind eyes. To me, he seemed way too young for this job. But he hadn't done anything that led me to believe he was incompetent.

Right now, the detective's intrusion was an answer to prayer.

Mostly because I wasn't prepared to talk to Weston again.

I didn't think of myself as fragile, but sometimes I feared I might be. I could put on a brave face, but that didn't change the fact that life had taught me lessons I hadn't wanted to learn.

"I'm really okay," I insisted, keeping my voice level. "Just embarrassed."

Detective Garrison's gaze traveled around the crowd. "Did anyone see anything? See who turned out the lights or knocked . . ." He looked at me as if searching for a name.

"Camryn. Camryn Paine."

"Who knocked Mrs. Paine down?" he finished.

Everyone shook their heads, confusion and cluelessness in their gazes.

My gaze fell on the camera that had been set up beside me, and I gasped. Right now, only a stand was there. "The camera . . ."

Everyone turned in the direction I pointed.

The video recorder was gone. It had been beside me. I'd just seen it there before the lights failed.

Someone had clearly pushed me down in order to grab it.

I paused for a minute, a conversation on the stage catching my ear.

The coroner spoke to another detective. One word stood out.

Asphyxiation.

That was the initial ruling on the cause of death.

I supposed that could tie in with Heather's peanut allergy.

But if that was the case, then why had someone grabbed the camera?

Unless there was evidence on it that might prove her death wasn't as simple as it appeared. Someone wouldn't have stolen the camera if Heather's death had been natural.

"The camera must have recorded something . . ." I muttered. "Maybe a clue about what happened."

Someone had turned the lights out, grabbed the camera, and run.

Only one person made sense as the culprit . . . the killer.

My breath caught, and I turned to Detective Garrison. If my theory was true, then the killer had a fatal flaw in his plans.

"I was taking a video of the rehearsal right before Heather died," I announced. "If there was anything on that other video, there's a good chance it's on my phone also."

"Is that right?" His eyes widened with intrigue.

"I'm going to need you to send me a copy of that recording."

***

"IT APPEARS we've dropped you right into the middle of the fire." Joseph took a long sip of his sparkling water. Sweat beaded on his forehead and wet his shirt beneath his arms. Some things hadn't changed.

Two hours had passed. The police had finally left Grand Isle's Hannon Auditorium. But they hadn't given any clues about what they thought had happened. I only knew about Heather's possible asphyxiation because of what I'd overheard.

Whatever the reason she'd died, a profound sense of sadness hung over the school.

"I just hate that this happened." I crossed my legs as I stared across the massive desk at Joseph, where he sat like a king on his throne. "We can meet later, if that's better for you."

"We'll probably have to. But there are a few things we need to go over now. The board will meet tonight to figure out if we should cancel the rest of Harvest Week because of this."

"That's understandable."

He shifted and leaned on his desk toward me. "The death of Velvet Matthews two weeks ago has been weighing heavily on us. Donors have been threatening to pull their support, which would put the school in a precarious position financially."

"You mean that tuition alone doesn't pay the bills?"

He let out a disdainful chuckle. "Not even close. There are definite challenges to being a private college. We still have some of the endowments we were previously given, but the board members are getting nervous that students are going to pull out of the school if the campus doesn't seem safe. I've already hired extra security. And now this . . ."

I frowned, hating the dilemma he was in—but hating the fact that students had died even more. "How would you like me to proceed?"

His face twitched as if he wanted to frown. "We'll need a press release."

"Of course. I think we should plan a candlelight vigil also. Something to pay our respects to Heather."

"That's an excellent idea. Could you head that up?"

"I'd be happy to."

Joseph's stormy gray eyes momentarily lightened

with gratitude. "Have I told you how glad I am that you're here?"

A smile tugged at my lips. "It feels like coming home."

His gaze seemed to darken a moment before he shifted in his seat. I knew this was weighing on him. Joseph had big shoes to fill after his father had passed five years ago. I could only imagine the pressure he was under.

Finally, he turned his gaze back to me. "I know you have a lot to do, Camryn. Let me introduce you to your assistant, Professor Skittles. She'll be able to help you with any questions you might have."

"Professor Skittles?" I tried not to gape, but I had no idea who he was talking about.

"She's the assistant for the public relations department. I'm sure she'll do whatever you need her to do."

He rose, opened his office door, and called to someone. A moment later, a girl with unusually bright red hair stepped inside, a huge smile on her face.

She wore knee-high socks that looked like a keyboard, a yellow boarding-school-style skirt that was about four inches too short, and a multicolored top. Bright blue plastic-framed glasses covering half her face perched on her nose, and her hair was pulled into two pigtails that were so short they almost looked like puppy dog ears.

"Camryn Paine," she rushed. "I'm so excited to meet you."

"You're a professor?" I continued to stare at her, unable to hide my confusion.

This girl looked thirteen. I'd fully expected to see a tenured staff member in my doorway.

"No, I legally changed my name. I now identify as a professor." She giggled as if her choice amused her.

I let out a breath, starting to understand a little better. "I see."

Yet I didn't. Not really.

I couldn't even begin to comprehend why she would do something like that—unless she liked attention. If that was the case, then I was going to have a massive issue working with her.

"Anyway, I'm a huge fan of yours. Like, *huge* huge. Like I think you're better than Adele, and *everyone* loves Adele." She held a wooden bowl full of purple candy. She popped a piece in her mouth as she grinned.

My throat tightened until I finally choked out, "Thank you."

"No, you don't understand. Your song 'Moon Over My Heart' is one of my all-time favorites." She started singing it.

I cringed—not because she was a bad singer but because the song drew too many memories.

I really wanted this conversation to be over. Based on the wide look in her eyes, that wouldn't be happening.

She abruptly stopped and studied me, her gaze traveling the length of me before she nodded with approval. "You know, you've *really* aged well. I figured you'd look ancient by now. But, looking at you, I would have guessed you were in your mid-thirties, not forty-something."

"Thanks . . . I think." Usually, I still felt young, like I should be in my twenties. Other times, reality reared its ugly head, and I clearly remembered all the years behind me.

"I was so bummed when you didn't put out any more albums after that first one—"

"I'm sorry to interrupt." Joseph stepped between us, his face pinched in a prudish expression. "But I'm sure you'll both have time to talk about this later. There are more important matters to discuss, yes?"

"Of course." Professor Skittles bent her head as if transforming into an obedient soldier.

"I look forward to working with you," I told her. "Maybe you can start by showing me to my office."

"Of course." Professor Skittles instantly perked as she raised her head. "Would you like me to do that now?"

I glanced back at Joseph, who nodded.

With a goodbye, I followed Professor Skittles to my office. It was located only a few doors down from Joseph's. Senior administrative staff had their own wing here at the college, separate from financial aid, admissions, and other departments.

But as I prepared myself to start this new chapter of my life, part of me wondered what exactly I'd gotten myself into. Had I moved from one bad situation directly into another?

That's how it felt at the moment.

But my old roommate's daughter had died, and I knew I wouldn't be able to rest until I had some answers. If this had happened to my own daughter . . . I could only imagine how horrific it would be.

For Rebecca's and Heather's sake, I would find answers.

CHAPTER FOUR

I DUTIFULLY STOOD at the side of the stage located in Epson Hall, lined up in a row with the conservatory's other key administrators, as Dr. Hannon addressed the faculty and staff.

As a performing arts music conservatory, the school had many theaters. The one where the talent show was supposed to take place was the largest, with an auditorium that seated five thousand.

The school had originally been started with an emphasis on classical music. But, several decades ago, board members had decided to expand musical genres in order to keep pace with today's culture. They'd added more academies within the conservatory: the academy of contemporary music, the academy of soul, and the academy of strategic music management.

Epson Hall was a part of the academy of strategic music management and was entirely less fancy and more outdated. Five hundred could be comfortably seated in this auditorium.

Right now, there weren't nearly that many.

Keeping my best professional demeanor, I watched as Joseph addressed everyone concerning today's incident. The perspiration on his water bottle matched the perspiration on his skin. He wiped his forehead with a handkerchief every few minutes. Three empty bottles of sparkling water sat on a shelf inside the wooden podium, and the small of his back appeared wet.

I could only imagine the fun students probably had with that trait of his.

I understood why Joseph needed to get a jump on this situation. News about what had happened would travel fast—as would rumors.

Our first priority, even before doing crisis management to the media, was to bring in grief counselors for Heather's friends and anyone else who might need help getting through this.

But there was a practical side to death also, things that couldn't be ignored. The aftermath, including informing family and friends, planning a funeral, tying up loose ends. Plus, I wasn't convinced her death was natural. I didn't care what anyone else said. My intuition told me that something had happened to cause Heather's demise.

Twenty-year-olds with peanut allergies knew to check labels on everything they ate. They knew to keep an EpiPen with them. Natural, untimely death scenes didn't include stealing a video recording.

Why was I the only one who could see this?

As I stood on the stage, I glanced out at the crowd.

The school had only thirty professors. Each academy accepted only one hundred students. But other staff members were also here. Security guards. Dorm parents. Cafeteria workers. Housekeepers. Academic assistants. Administration.

Altogether, probably a hundred people were in the room right now.

Each looked shellshocked as they heard the news about Heather's death. But Joseph didn't present the situation as a crime. Everyone was sweeping this under the rug, weren't they?

If this was anything but a natural death, then things wouldn't look good for Grand Isle Conservatory. Joseph knew that. He was trying to put his own spin on the situation.

Putting spins on things was my job.

As soon as Joseph ended his meeting, everyone stood and began to murmur amongst each other. I walked down the steps and searched out the faces of those around me, looking for any signs of guilt.

My dad always told me I had an eye for reading people.

Then again, if that was true, wouldn't I have predicted that my father might end up in jail one day?

Life was full of so many ironic moments.

I paused and listened to everything going on around me.

The footsteps—some crisp, some muted. The voices whispering and comforting. The clock ticking on the wall. The sound guy wrapping up cords on the stage.

My brother had said hearing was my superpower. Sometimes, it felt more like a curse. But I'd learned to control my acute abilities so I could function.

I'd go crazy if I didn't.

"I thought that was you," someone behind me said.

Without turning, I knew exactly who had approached me. I plastered on a soft smile as I pivoted. "Jinky Jennings!"

My former classmate was now a voice professor at the conservatory—a real professor, not just someone who identified as one.

She looked as flamboyant as ever. That was the best word I could think of to describe Jinky.

Her hair was just as blonde as ever and had been styled away from her face in big curls that seemed too old a style for someone her age. Her overwhelming pungent perfume filled my nostrils and took my breath away for a moment. That wasn't to mention the fact that I was nearly blinded by her red lipstick and fingernails.

Altogether, it was sensory overload—especially when I heard earrings jangling, the beads atop her dressy flip-flops clacking, and her gum smacking.

She threw her arms around me, her bright blue kimono stretching across her shoulders like a blanket. "Don't you look wonderful."

Jinky stepped back and practically beamed as she looked at me. She was a beamer. It was just what she did.

"Thank you. I can't believe I'm back here," I told her. "It seems surreal."

"Why *did* you come back here?" She studied my face as if she wanted some dirt from me.

"Joseph offered me the opportunity, and I just felt like life was going to come full circle." Plus, he'd sounded desperate, *and* there was nothing I loved more than a good challenge.

"I heard that saying no to opportunities makes us age faster."

"Really? I've never heard that."

"I'm pretty much obsessed with teaching myself —that old dog—some new tricks. I read up on everything I can. Anyway . . ." She nodded before moving on. "It's almost as if the old gang is back together again, isn't it? I'm here, Joseph is still here, Weston's here, and now you."

As she said Weston's name, my gaze wandered behind her. I'd seen him sitting in the audience, and I wondered what he was doing now.

Was he charming people? He was a master at getting people to like him, something I'd been jealous about on more than one occasion.

My throat went dry when I saw Detective Garrison step into the room. He paused at the back doors and glanced around as if searching for someone.

Did he have an update? Or did he have more questions to ask someone?

Otherwise, why would he be here?

After a moment, he walked toward Weston. The detective whispered something to Weston, and Weston immediately tensed. He nodded at Garrison before the two of them exited the room together.

"What do you think that's about?" I murmured as I followed them with my gaze.

Jinky raised her thin eyebrows and shrugged. "Hard to say. But I know that Heather really thought a lot of Weston."

Her words caught me off guard, and I glanced up at her. Her tone had lifted as she said the words, almost as if she wanted to dangle a worm in front of me and hook my curiosity. There was clearly more to her statement.

But what exactly was the subtext of that statement? Had Heather had a crush on Weston?

I figured there was no need to beat around the bush. When I realized that half my life could nearly be over, I'd decided I was too old to play games. The realization was incredibly freeing.

"What does that mean?" I asked.

Jinky shrugged again. "It doesn't mean anything

specifically. I just know some students here have a big crush on Professor Turner."

"But he's not the type who'd lead them on or do anything inappropriate, right?" That wasn't the Weston I knew. How had he changed in the years since we'd been the Dynamic Duo?

"Weston always gets plenty of female attention—age hasn't changed that. Does he miss his old days in the limelight when women would throw themselves at him? I don't know. But I think he's too smart to strike up anything with a student."

Relief filled me. I wasn't sure why. But I didn't want to think of Weston as that type.

"Then again, do we ever really know anybody?" Jinky let out a sigh.

Her words hung in the air, and I knew I'd be thinking about them for the rest of the night.

"SO, HOW'S EVERYTHING GOING?" Professor Skittles walked beside me as I headed to my office after the meeting. She'd insisted on escorting me. "Is it weird to be back here?"

"This place is just like I remember it." My statement seemed safe. The campus really hadn't changed much.

"Isn't it beautiful here? I just love it. I mean, I don't love what happened today. But I love this place." She threw her hands in the air, and I could almost imagine a rainbow spreading between her fingertips and into the air.

"What academy are you in?" I asked, figuring I might as well get to know her.

"Contemporary. Pop, to be specific. I'm actually a huge fan of K-pop."

"Korean pop music?" The music genre had originated in South Korea and contained a mix of hip-hop, electronic dance, jazz, and rock. Usually, it was performed in groups. One of Scarlett's friends was a huge fan.

Professor Skittles eagerly nodded. "That's right. That's my life goal one day."

"Well, it's good to have goals."

As we walked along the sidewalk, with willow trees offering shade from the October sun, my thoughts drifted back to Heather. I wanted to find out more about her. Maybe Skittles would have some answers.

But before the questions could leave my lips, something slithered in front of us.

Professor Skittles grabbed my arm and jumped back. "Oh, my goodness, it's a snake! A snake! I hate snakes!"

I glanced down at the critter—a small green snake, probably less than a foot long. "It's okay, stay calm."

"Stay calm? I can't stay calm." She hid behind me. With every new word she spoke, her pitch climbed into another level—a sure sign of panic. "What do they tell you to do when you see a snake? Stop, drop, and roll, right?"

I tried not to gawk at her question. *This* girl was going to be my assistant?

"No, that's when there's a fire." I continued watching as the snake disappeared into a flower bed. "It's gone now."

Professor Skittles peeked around me before she took my arm and hurried me past the area, still clearly in panic mode. "I hate snakes. I just *hate* them. When I was a little girl, I was walking with my parents when one fell out of a tree and onto my shoulders. I've been traumatized ever since."

"I'm sorry to hear that, but whatever you do, please don't stop, drop, and roll when you see a snake."

She seemed like a full-time job in herself. But I

reminded myself to be patient. I'd been a full-time job at one time also.

Professor Skittles fanned her face with her hand. "I know. When I get nervous, I get my advice mixed up. That's not a good thing."

"I can imagine."

As we stepped inside the admin building, she turned to me and clasped her hands beneath her chin. "Well, I can't wait to work with you, Mrs. Paine. We're so excited to have you with us."

"Thank you." I paused, questions lingering in my head. I still wanted more information about Heather. Was it uncouth to ask Skittles about her? I wasn't sure.

But I needed to seize this opportunity.

I called to Professor Skittles before she walked away. "By the way, were you friends with Heather Klein?"

She turned back to me, and her expression instantly sobered. "I wouldn't say we were friends. I'm a freshman, and she was a junior. She was studying classical music, and, like I said, my dream is to be in a K-Pop band. But we did talk a few times. She seemed nice."

"Did anyone have any reason to hurt her?"

Professor Skittles tilted her head. "Hurt her? You don't think this was an accident?"

I swallowed hard. "Working PR, I need to consider every possibility. It's just a question."

That seemed to appease her, and she nodded slowly, thoughtfully. "I wish I could tell you something. I have no idea. But I know I'll be sleeping with my door locked and a chair in front of it tonight."

That sounded like a good idea, even though I knew the police were working hard on this.

In times of murder, every precaution should be taken.

And until we learned how Heather died, it was best to think of this as a worst-case scenario.

CHAPTER FIVE

I PULLED my oversized bag up higher on my shoulder as I hurried down the steps from the admin building and headed toward the sidewalk.

What a day.

Joseph had called Heather's family, and they were coming to town. They wouldn't arrive until tomorrow since they lived in Colorado and had to arrange flights. That would give Joseph and me some time to sort things out before they came.

For now, I headed to my apartment. Though I'd been offered on-campus housing, I'd found my own place within walking distance of the campus.

Thankfully, the weather was good today, if not a bit humid. But what did I expect in Savannah? Even though it was October, humidity still lingered.

As did snakes, apparently.

I shook my head when I remembered Professor Skittles' reaction earlier today. The girl was definitely a character.

As I glanced around the campus at the massive oak trees that were draped in moss, I couldn't help but smile. In the distance, a quartet practiced jazz music. The whole atmosphere almost made me feel like I'd been transported to New Orleans. But this place was far from the Big Easy.

As I continued down the sidewalk, I heard a door open in the distance. I expected students to flood outside to hit some nightlife. Instead, Weston sauntered out. His confident swagger, his barely there beard, and urban cowboy clothing made him look like he'd just stepped from a music video.

Our gazes met again, and we both seemed to freeze.

But Weston's surprised expression lasted only a moment. A slow smile spread across his face, and he picked up his pace as he headed toward me, his cowboy boots clicking across the cobblestones.

"Fancy running into you," he said.

I gripped the bag at my shoulder and tried to remain composed. But a flash of pre-adolescent thrill rushed through me, though I willed the feeling to disappear. "I had no idea you were here at Grand Isle."

"You mean you haven't kept up with me through all these years?" He grinned as he fell into step beside me.

"Tempting, but no."

"Ouch." His hand went up over his heart, but his grin indicated he was just kidding. "It's really great to see you, Camryn. It's been a long time."

"Yes, it has. You're looking good also. It seems like working here at the school really suits you."

He glanced up at the building as we passed it. The architecture of the entire campus was Gothic and had been designed to fit in with the feel of the city. There were uncountable arches, flying buttresses, and stained-glass windows that gave the campus a classic feel.

"I love it here," he said. "I didn't think teaching would be this fulfilling when I'm so used to being onstage. But I feel like maybe I've found my calling."

The school asked that former students come back and teach for a year as their way of giving back. A surprising number of graduates followed through. Was that why he'd returned?

"That's great," I said. "I'm really glad to hear that."

After a brief moment of silence, Weston spoke again, his tone more subdued this time. "Listen, I'm really sorry to hear about Phil."

I quickly shook my head at the name of my deceased husband. "Thank you. It was a shock."

His gaze softened. "I can only imagine. How's your daughter doing? Scarlett, right?"

"Yes, Scarlett. We're both hanging in. She started college a couple of months ago, and I think the change of scenery has been good for her. Our old house was feeling awfully big and empty."

"I can imagine. Did she get her mom's singing chops? Part of me wondered if she might come here to Grand Isle."

I smiled when I thought about my daughter with her determined gaze and bright smile. She was the perfect mix of me and Phil. She had my passion and her father's smarts.

"She can sing, that's for sure," I said. "And she has a great stage presence. But Scarlett claims she wants to go into business like her dad."

Surprise flashed through his gaze. "Well, to each her own, right?"

"That's how the saying goes."

We walked for a few minutes in silence until we

finally reached the edge of campus where the faculty parking lot was located.

"Is your car around here?" Weston asked.

A knot formed in my throat. "No, it's not. I actually rented an apartment within walking distance. It's just a couple of blocks down."

"How about if I walk with you? Would that be too strange?"

I wanted to scream yes, it would be strange—entirely too strange. But I sensed Weston was trying to be polite. This had nothing to do with our past relationship and everything to do with simply being a decent human.

"You don't have to do that," I finally said.

"There's been some crime in this area lately, and it's getting dark. I'd feel better if you let me."

Fighting the offer would be a waste of energy. Weston and I were going to be working together, even though I planned on avoiding him as much as possible.

"Why not then?" I finally said with a shrug.

We paced silently beside each other before Weston said, "It was a crazy day today, wasn't it?"

The conversation felt entirely too mundane considering a student had died. But I knew where he was coming from.

"I can't believe Heather just died like that," I said. "I can't wrap my mind around it. I can only imagine what Rebecca and her husband are going through."

"I know. I can't imagine either. Heather was such a sweet girl. In fact, she reminded me a little bit of you. She was talented, but she didn't love being the center of attention. Of course, you've always been naturally gifted. Heather had to work at it more."

"If she got into school here, then she must have had decent talent."

"Yes, except sometimes she let herself get in the way." Weston shrugged. "We can be our own worst enemies sometimes, can't we?"

I let out a chuckle. "I can understand that."

So many questions ran through my head. Questions about Weston's failed marriage. About the past several years of his life. About why he'd really ended up coming back here and about why he was still here.

Maybe I'd have a chance to ask later. Maybe I wouldn't. Life would go on either way.

I glanced ahead at the cobblestone street and spotted my apartment. My place wasn't that far away now. Maybe I could insist on walking the rest of the way alone.

But as I cleared my throat and started to launch

into my explanation, I heard footsteps rushing from behind. Heard heavy, quick breathing.

The next instant, I felt someone beside me.

I glanced over just in time to see a masked man grab my purse and dart away.

CHAPTER SIX

THE MAN nearly knocked me off my feet in his scramble to get away. I stumbled into Weston as the breath left my lungs.

Weston caught me before yelling after the man, "Hey!"

He started to dash after the thief, but I grabbed his arm, holding him here. "No, it's not worth it. Nowadays, you just don't know where confrontations will lead. I'll just call the police."

He gripped my arm and glanced in the direction of the man who'd disappeared from sight. Finally, Weston's shoulders softened with resignation as he turned back to me and studied my expression.

"Are you sure you're okay?"

Even though I was shaken, I nodded. "Second

time someone shoved me today. That might be a record."

Weston's eyes glimmered. "A record? I doubt that. I remember all those fans who shoved everyone around, desperate to get closer to you when you did those autograph sessions while you were on tour. You always hated that."

I frowned. "Yes, I did. I prefer not to go back to those days."

"You don't miss the attention?"

"Not one bit." In fact, the thought of being jostled by crowds, being jetted off from one place to another, of losing all privacy made hives break out across my skin. "How about you?"

He shrugged. "I miss it sometimes."

I stared at him a moment before snapping out of my daze. Instead, I reached for my cell phone so I could call the police—except I realized I didn't have my bag any longer. "Oh, I can't call them."

"The police? Let me." Weston grabbed the phone from his pocket and dialed. A few minutes later, after he explained the situation, he said, "The police want to know if you can go into the station. It's right around the corner. You can give your statement there."

"Of course."

"We'll be right there," he said into the phone before disconnecting.

It looked like I was going to need to be around Weston a little longer.

This day seemed to just be getting worse and worse.

———

AFTER I FINISHED FILLING out the report at the police station, I rose from the desk where I'd been seated, ready to finally get back to my apartment.

But while I was here . . . I scanned the place, looking for Garrison.

The station was small with only about eight desks set up in the center of an open room. I hadn't seen the detective when I arrived, but as I searched the room now, I saw him stride inside through a back entrance and pause by a desk in the corner.

"What are you thinking?" Weston asked as he stood beside me.

I shrugged. "While we're here . . ."

"You want to talk to Garrison?"

"Why not?"

As we walked across the room, my thoughts shifted to my purse again. I had little hope the cops would actually recover it. That meant that, after I left here, I'd need to cancel my credit cards and buy a new phone—without thus said credit card.

Considering I'd just moved here, the timing couldn't be worse. I hadn't had time to unpack or stash any money away, and I still needed to purchase several things, starting with some groceries.

But I'd figure that out later.

As we approached Garrison, I paused. The officer at the desk next to him was playing the video I'd taken right before Heather died. My blood felt cold as I listened to it.

"Mrs. Paine?" Garrison straightened when he saw me. "What are you doing here?"

I explained to him what had happened, and he grunted at the update, keeping any opinions to himself.

That was fine.

But I had a question for him. "I don't want to overstep, but how's the investigation into Heather's death going?"

A frown tugged at his lips. "We're still waiting for the medical examiner to pinpoint the exact cause of her death."

"In the meantime, are you treating this as a homicide?"

He raised his eyebrows. "A homicide? It was a suspicious death, at best. But I wouldn't go as far as to say it was a murder."

"But someone stole the video camera."

Garrison nodded. "Right, but how is that related to her death? Most likely, it was a criminal seizing an opportunity."

I tried not to gawk at the absurdity of his statement. "You and I both know that video camera couldn't have been worth much. Maybe there was something recorded there that someone didn't want anyone to see."

"She has a good point." Weston stepped closer. "Did any of the other cameras around the school catch who's responsible for stealing the video recorder? If you can find this guy, maybe you can find more answers."

Garrison's neck tightened. "The security cameras were all vandalized. The school is working to get them replaced."

I processed that for a minute before asking, "Someone vandalized those cameras before Heather died?"

Garrison's cheek twitched. "It actually happened last week. We don't believe the crimes are related— more like some kids up to mischief."

I didn't believe in coincidences—in most cases, at least. I thought he was being entirely too optimistic. But sometimes you had to know when to back off, and this was one of those times. I couldn't push too hard.

Before I stepped away, I paused as something on the video caught my ear. "Did you hear that?"

Garrison stared at me as if I'd lost my mind. "Hear what?"

"A whoosh." I pointed at the screen on the desk next to his. "Right before Heather died, there was a whoosh, like a door opened in the auditorium."

Garrison glanced over at the officer, his eyes still narrow as if skeptical about my words. "Rewind that."

The officer did as Garrison said and replayed the last thirty seconds.

I held my breath until he reached the spot where I'd heard the noise. Then I snapped my fingers. "Right there! A door opened about six seconds before Heather died."

Garrison still shook his head. "I don't know what you're hearing that I'm not. I definitely didn't hear a door opening."

"If Camryn says she heard it, it's there." Weston's hands went to his hips as he stepped closer. "Is there a way you can isolate certain noises in the background? On TV they make it look both possible and easy."

"I can see what we can do." Garrison stared at me, not bothering to hide his curiosity. He might even be a little impressed. "But how did you pick up on that sound when none of the rest of us did?"

I shrugged, not wanting to make a big deal of my abilities. "I have a few hidden talents."

"Don't let her fool you. She's practically a savant when it comes to these things." A touch of admiration stretched through Weston's voice. "Cam can hear things no one else can. She can emulate the exact note you want to hear—can pull it from thin air. Her talents are actually amazing."

Garrison stared at me for another moment, interest gleaming in his eyes. "Is that right?"

I shrugged, wishing that Weston hadn't made such a big deal about it. Sometimes people got weird about my skills or thought my abilities were almost freakish. I'd heard it all.

"Everything I hear can either be a blessing or a curse, depending on the day," I finally said, trying to close the conversation down before it went any further.

The detective nodded to a room in the distance.

"Would you mind going in there and listening to the video away from all the other sounds here at the station? Who knows what else you might hear?"

I only had to think about his request a moment before nodding. Heather's death and finding the girl's killer was more important than anything else I had to do.

Because I was certain Heather's death wasn't accidental or natural. Someone somehow had managed to kill her while she stood alone on the stage.

"I'd be more than happy to." I turned to Weston, realizing he'd already taken an hour out of his day because of me. "I don't want to make you wait around any longer. I'm sure you have other things to do."

Knowing Weston, he probably had a girlfriend waiting at home for him. He'd probably charmed her with his croon-worthy voice, and now she giggled at everything he said.

And she was probably twenty-five years old —tops.

I hated to be so jaded, but I'd been around the block a few times.

"I don't mind waiting with you." Weston

shrugged as if he had all the time in the world. "In fact, I'd feel better if I did."

I nibbled on my bottom lip before saying, "Are you sure?"

"Of course. You shouldn't be alone after what just happened. I'll stick around and walk you home."

It looked like I wouldn't be getting rid of him anytime soon.

One part of me wished I could shoo him away. But another part was happy he was still around.

When hard times came, having someone to offer you support was always nice. I just wished that the someone wasn't the man who'd broken my heart.

CHAPTER SEVEN

I HIT the Pause button on the video player and then backed up the footage so I could listen again. "There it is. Did you guys hear it?"

Everyone in the room stared at me with blank expressions on their faces.

By everyone, I meant Detective Garrison; his colleague, Detective Bateman; and the department's audio specialist, Dan Hardy.

"Is there any way you could turn up the gain?" I asked Dan.

He made a few adjustments before hitting Play again. This time, the sound of a door opening was clearer. Even the people around me seemed to hear it.

"What if that was the killer stepping inside to see if his or her plan worked?" I asked.

"His or her plan?" Garrison stared at me, a cautiously irritated look in his eyes.

"Twenty-year-olds don't just drop dead," I continued. "What if Heather was poisoned? There are poisons that would cause her throat to tighten. Something could have happened right before she went onstage and—"

"First of all, we don't know she was killed." Garrison raised his chin as if challenging me to defy him again. "And, secondly, if someone had stepped into the auditorium—which was closed to everyone except the crew and the person warming up—someone would have seen him or her."

"Not necessarily," I said. "It was dark in there. Besides, if there was a killer . . . maybe the killer was someone who blended in with everyone else who was at rehearsals."

"That's a big claim, Mrs. Paine." Garrison gave me a fatherly look, which annoyed me since he was nearly young enough to be my son—if I'd been a teen mom.

"I just think there's more here than meets the eye."

Garrison rose, clearly done with this conversation and maybe even becoming territorial about this investigation. "I assure you that we're working every angle. We hope to have some answers soon. Thank you, in the meantime, for all you've done."

I nodded to the detective, hating feeling like I was being dismissed. But there was nothing else I could do or say right now. "If there's anything else you need, just give me a call."

"If your purse turns up, we'll let you know."

Neither Weston nor I said anything until we stepped outside.

That was when I realized I'd also lost the key to my apartment when my purse was stolen. I closed my eyes, fighting frustration.

"What is it?" Weston lowered his voice, and I knew by the direction of his tone that he was facing me.

"I don't have a key to get into my apartment, and I haven't been here for long enough to give anyone else a backup copy."

"Hopefully, the building manager can get you a new one. Let's go see."

I didn't argue with him as he started walking with me toward my apartment building. The street suddenly didn't feel quite as quaint and welcome as it did earlier this evening.

"You're going to have a lot to do once you get back, aren't you?" Weston glanced over at me as we moseyed down the sidewalk. Moseyed seemed like the best word for it considering the way Weston's hands were tucked casually in his pockets and the slow click of his cowboy boots.

"Unfortunately, I don't even have a phone or a way to buy a new phone." I let out a breath and ran a hand through my hair as my headache pounded harder.

"I'm sorry. I can only imagine how frustrating this can be. Let me help you get some things figured out. I have a cell phone and a credit card you can use if you need them."

My throat tightened at his words, at the thought of spending more time with him. I wasn't sure how I felt about it, but everything inside me told me I should probably flee. "You've already done so much."

Weston paused and turned toward me, his eyes warm as they locked onto mine. "Look, you're new in town. Just let me do this for you. Okay?"

I stared at him a moment, trying to figure out if I should dig my heels in and claim independence or if I should admit that I needed help.

Finally, I nodded. "Okay. Thank you, and I appreciate it."

A few minutes later, we found the manager, who gave me a key despite the fact that I didn't have any ID on me. Weston's ability to charm people had paid off. The manager almost promised to change my locks tomorrow. Until then, I'd be utilizing my deadbolt to try to maintain a sense of safety while I was sleeping.

I trudged up to the second floor where my tiny apartment was located. As I stuck the key in the lock and opened the door, I glanced at Weston. I knew I wasn't going to get rid of him this easily. So when he stepped inside, I didn't say anything.

"Nice place." He scanned the small, six hundred-square-foot apartment.

I glanced around, liking my temporary home too. It had come fully furnished and had lots of interesting angles and nooks. Plus, a wrought iron-balcony jutted from patio doors off the living room and made me feel like I'd been swept into another time and place.

"I thought it was charming."

"It reminds me of the house you used to always talk about wanting to get. You had such romantic notions about the future, all the way down to having a balcony so you could be serenaded and an English garden."

A sad smile pulled at my lips. "Yes, I did, didn't I?"

I'd assumed that Weston had forgotten about that. That he had forgotten about me.

But, apparently, that wasn't the case.

As he turned back to me, I caught a whiff of his familiar cologne. The aroma was musky and clean and leathery. All the best combinations, in my opinion.

As I caught myself taking another whiff, I quickly stepped back and mentally scolded myself.

"Listen, how about if I go pick up a new phone for you?" Weston asked.

My spirits lifted for a moment before crashing again. The idea was tempting. But the last thing I needed was to owe Weston anything. The more distance I could keep from the man, the better.

"That's really nice of you to offer," I started. "But it's going to take a while for me to work things out with my bank and—"

"You can pay me back later."

I stared at him a moment and tried to figure out what the best response was. But the more I thought about it, the more I realized I didn't have many options right now. Especially since I didn't have a car.

"If you wouldn't mind doing that, it would be amazing," I finally said. "My hands are tied unless I'm able to use a phone to cancel my cards."

"I'd be more than happy to help." He glanced at his watch. "If I hurry, I can still make it to the store before it closes at nine."

"I appreciate that. Thank you again."

"Anything for you."

But his words hung in the air. That was his line. It was what he said. It was one of the reasons he'd first captured my heart all those years ago.

I looked away, unsure what my expression would tell him right now. Would he see remorse? Heartbreak? Betrayal?

I didn't know, but I didn't want to address it now.

Instead, I'd wait for him to come back with my phone, and while he was gone, I'd make a list of everything I needed to do.

BY THE TIME Weston returned to my apartment, I'd made a list of more than twenty tasks I needed to get done as soon as I had a phone. I had credit cards to cancel, a driver's license to obtain, insurance cards to duplicate.

What a headache.

He victoriously held up a bag in his hand. "Success."

He handed it to me, and I pulled out the box inside. The prepaid cell phone was just what I needed until I could get a new one from my carrier. "You're a real lifesaver."

He shrugged and lowered himself into the seat across from me. "What can I say? I try."

I rose and paced over to my coffeepot, grabbed an empty cup, and turned back to Weston. "Coffee?"

I hadn't bought groceries yet, but I *had* brought coffee with me. There were some things I knew I couldn't live without.

"I'd love some," he said.

"Black?" That was the way he used to drink it.

"There's no other way."

I poured him a cup and placed it on the table in front of him. Then I lowered myself back into my chair and took a sip of my own drink.

I paused and studied Weston a moment, trying to ignore the ocean of memories that stretched between us. "Can I ask you a question?"

"Go ahead."

I wasn't sure it was a good idea to broach the subject. But finding out answers about Heather still seemed better than thinking about my past with Weston.

"The other contestants for the talent show were waiting in the lobby, right?" I started.

He nodded, almost seeming hesitant. "That's right."

"Who are the frontrunners?"

He let out a breath. "You know everyone who comes to Grand Isle is incredibly talented."

"But there are always a few who rise to the top."

"You're right. There are." He let out another breath. "If I had to pick, I'd say Beck Tarsus. He writes his own songs and has a bit of an Adam Levine sound. Also, Jordan Sawyer. He's a rapper and spoken word artist. He's incredible."

"Anyone else?"

Weston let out another long breath. "There's a student named Jana Littleton. Everyone says she's going to be the new Alanis Morissette. If I had to pick, those are the three best."

"Did I understand correctly that Jordan broke his arm, Jana recently got food poisoning, and Beck was in a car accident?"

Weston's throat tightened. "That's correct."

I made mental notes. "What about Heather? Was she a front-runner?"

He shrugged. "Maybe she was fourth or fifth on the list. Her nerves were getting the best of her yesterday. Apparently, she's been distracted lately."

"I wonder why." Did it somehow tie in with her murder? Maybe she'd received a threat or the other accidents on campus had spooked her.

"I couldn't tell you."

I continued taking mental notes. Had another show front-runner done something to the competition?

I didn't know, but it seemed like a possibility.

"Just one more question." I hesitated before asking, but there was no stopping me now. "Why did Detective Garrison talk to you after Hannon's meeting with the faculty and staff?"

As soon as the question left my lips, a shadow covered Weston's face. He shifted. Or was that a cringe? I wasn't sure. But the question clearly made him uncomfortable.

"It was nothing. We were just chatting about the talent show. Why are you asking?"

"Because I'm going to need to get to the bottom of what's happening here."

He narrowed his eyes and tilted his head in

confusion. "What do you mean *you're going to need to get to the bottom of this*? You work public relations. You're not a cop."

I squared my shoulders. "Part of public relations is establishing a positive image in the community for my clients. Having a suspicious death hanging over the school is one of the worst reputations that Grand Isle could have. That means I need to figure out what's going on."

Weston nodded slowly before shaking his head. "I'm not sure you investigating Heather's death is a good idea. You don't know what you're getting yourself into."

Something about his words sounded ominous. He knew more than he was letting on, didn't he? But what exactly did he know?

I knew one thing now. Weston wasn't going to share any more information with me. Not now.

As if reading my mind, he suddenly stood. "Look, I know you have a lot to do so I'm going to get going. But I'd love to catch up another time."

I watched as he backed away, clearly eager for an excuse to leave.

That was fine by me because I needed an excuse to be by myself.

"Thanks again for everything," I told him as he turned toward the door. "I'll talk to you later."

With a wave, Weston was gone.

As silence stretched around me, I started a new list.

This one contained items that I needed to look into concerning Heather's death.

Because if this had been Scarlett, I'd want someone to help me.

CHAPTER EIGHT

AS I LAY in bed that night, I couldn't sleep.

I decided to call Scarlett. She answered on the first ring, her voice breathless. Crowds sounded in the background—as if she were at a party—and she spoke loudly to be heard over them. "Hello?"

"Hi, honey. It's Mom. I had to get a new phone today."

"Mom! I was hoping you'd call."

I frowned as I leaned back against my headboard. I'd feared when Scarlett left for college that she might get into the party and drinking scene. Even though I'd talked to her and tried to explain what the consequences could be for poor choices, I knew those things were almost a right-of-passage once kids went to college.

It was just one more reason I prayed for her every single day. I'd started from the time she was in my womb.

"Why'd you get a new phone?" Scarlett asked.

"It's a long story." I baulked as I tried to tune out the overwhelming noises zinging through the other end of the phone line. "I feel like I'm interrupting something."

"Don't be silly. I'm just out with my friends."

"Sounds like you're having a good time." I remembered Heather and swallowed the knot in my throat. "I just wanted to hear your voice. Everything okay?"

"Yes . . . I mean, yes." Her second yes held much more enthusiasm than the first, and clearly sounded forced.

"What's going on?" I didn't need to have special auditory abilities to know there was something on her mind.

The sounds in the background muted a moment, and I pictured Scarlett stepping away from the crowds.

"I wanted to mention one thing to you." Scarlett hesitated. "There's this boy . . ."

In my gut, I knew this wasn't about "some boy" she liked. There was more to this.

"I think he's following me," she muttered.

I sucked in a breath and sat up straighter in bed. "What do you mean?"

"I mean, wherever I go, I see him there. But he never talks to me. It's kind of creeping me out."

Another image of Heather filled my mind. "Have you told anyone else?"

"No, I don't want to overreact."

"It's not overreacting. You need to tell your dorm mom. Security too. It's better to be safe than sorry, as the saying goes."

"But..."

"I mean it, Scarlett. Do you want me to come pick you up?"

"No! No." Her voice changed from panicked to purposefully calm. "I was afraid to say anything to you."

I frowned as her words cut into my heart. "I want you to be able to tell me anything."

"I know. But you're overreacting."

I forced my voice into a more peaceful tone, one that wouldn't scare her off from talking to me in the future. It was such a delicate balance sometimes, and I wished that Phil was here to help me navigate these waters.

"I'll try to do better. I just worry about you."

Especially considering what had happened at Grand Isle. I didn't tell her that, though.

"I know, Mom. I love you. And I'll be careful. I promise."

I wanted to say I felt better or reassured at her words. But I didn't.

She was twelve hours away from me in New York City. I just couldn't hop into my car, even if I had one, and go check on her.

She was my baby. She always would be.

More than anything, I wanted to protect her right now.

<hr>

BETWEEN HEATHER'S DEATH, my conversation with Scarlett, and drinking coffee too late, I couldn't sleep.

Instead, I sat in bed and glanced at the box beside me. On top, I saw the old yearbook from my senior year at Grand Isle.

Of the few things I'd brought with me, this was one of them.

Most of my belongings were still in the stately house Phil and I had called home.

We'd lived in Atlanta, a good five hours from

here. I had a friend who would keep an eye on the place while I was gone. I couldn't bring myself to sell it yet, especially since I didn't know where I was going to end up. Plus, I had so many memories there. And if I sold the place . . .

Warm tears flooded my eyes. I just wasn't sure I was ready to do that yet. It would be a definitive closure on that chapter of my life, a chapter filled with so many sweet memories . . .

My assignment here would probably last a few months until I decided my next steps.

I leaned against my headboard, pillows propped behind me, and began flipping through the pages.

I stopped when I reached a picture of Jennifer Winant.

She'd been one of my classmates.

Two months before we were supposed to graduate, she disappeared.

To my knowledge, to this day no one had heard from her. No clues about what happened to her had ever turned up.

But her disappearance had haunted the school for years, putting the media spotlight on the college and the famous graduates it turned out.

Jennifer had gone out with friends the night

before she disappeared. She'd decided to stay late at a bar and walk home. Her friends had agreed.

Her roommate verified that Jennifer had finally returned around two in the morning. Her roommate had heard her come in.

Then the next morning, Jennifer was gone, never to be heard from again.

Jinky, Joseph, Weston, and I had been four of her closest friends. We hadn't been with her that night. We'd been working on a special project for one of our music classes. Jennifer had gone out with some other girls in our class instead.

I often wondered how things would be different if we'd been with her that night.

Would she still be around now?

I closed the yearbook and frowned.

Jinky, Joseph, Weston, and I were back together, and now another tragedy had happened on campus the very day I arrived.

I wanted to believe that was a coincidence. What else could it be? There were clearly no connections between today's event and my arrival on campus. Still . . . the timing felt eerie.

I reminded myself that other incidents *had* happened before I arrived. I wasn't sure if that made me feel better or worse.

I'd thought about Jennifer often over the years. I wondered where she was. If she was alive. What had happened to her.

Either way, it seemed like tragedy haunted Grand Isle. I didn't know how to change that.

Instead, I put the yearbook away.

I had some phone calls to make concerning my stolen wallet, and then I really needed to get some sleep. If tomorrow was anything like today, then I had my work cut out for me.

CHAPTER NINE

AS I HEADED to my office the next morning, exhaustion pulled at me.

I'd been on the phone half the night trying to cancel credit cards and figure out ways to buy groceries. My bank was overnighting me a new debit card, so that made me feel better.

But it didn't help me feel more awake.

I couldn't stop thinking about Heather's parents. About what they might be going through.

Hearing the news of their daughter's death had to be so awful.

Being away from Scarlett for the first time in my life had made my prayers more fervent. That was for sure. Now with the news of Heather, my prayers had doubled.

Scarlett was all I had left in the world. The life I'd built with Phil was gone. If I were to lose my daughter . . .

My throat burned with emotion.

I had to stop thinking like that.

I had almost made it into my office when Professor Skittles skipped up next to me. "Good morning, Mrs. Paine."

"Good morning." I glanced at the student, who'd dressed in an almost identical outfit today as yesterday. Personally, it reminded me of a clown, but to each their own. "You can call me Camryn."

"Really? Okay then, *Camryn*." She said my name with lots of special effects, her voice lilting up to a G sharp before wavering into a nervous giggle. She reached into that wooden bowl she held and snatched an orange piece of candy.

My new assistant was very interesting, to say the least.

"I heard the board didn't make a decision yet about the rest of Harvest Week," Skittles announced.

"That's not surprising," I said. "I'm sure they're all still trying to process what happened."

I'd told Joseph that, in my opinion, they should delay the event instead of canceling it. I hadn't been invited to the meeting last night, however, which was fine by me.

I turned back to Skittles.

"Are you working for me this morning?" I still wasn't clear what our schedule was.

I paused by my office door, keys in hand, and waited for her to answer.

"My normal hours are Mondays, Wednesdays, and Fridays from nine a.m. until one. I hope that works for you. I can squeeze in some extra time this week if you need me to. You know, with everything going on and all."

"Of course." I turned away from my door and scanned the admin area in front of the offices. No one else was nearby. Perfect. "First order of business today: do you know if we have access to student records?"

She shrugged. "I'm not really sure."

"I need you to find out for me. Then I need you to get me Heather Klein's file."

"You mean, if they tell me we *do* have access *then* you want me to get her file?"

I gave her a pointed look but said nothing. After a few seconds, her eyes widened as she caught my drift.

"Oh . . . that's *not* what you mean, is it?" A grin slowly spread across her face. "I like the way you think."

"I appreciate your help on this. And I appreciate your discretion on the matter as well."

Skittles nodded, almost a little too quickly. "Of course." She started to take a step away when she paused. "Can I ask you a question, Mrs.—I mean, Camryn?"

"You can ask, and I might answer."

She giggled, almost nervously this time. "I like that you're direct . . . I think."

"What's your question, Professor Skittles?" It pained me to say her full name for some reason. I felt like I was giving her respect she hadn't earned, even if it was just a nickname.

I was overthinking it, though, and had bigger issues to worry about.

"Did you really have stage fright?" Skittles lowered her voice. "Is that why you only put out one album?"

Her question was about my old music career. Of course.

I shook my head. "I walked away because I was living somebody else's dream instead of my own."

"Wasn't that hard? I mean, isn't fame the pinnacle of success and what everybody wants?"

I locked gazes with her. "If there's one thing I've learned, it's this. Not every opportunity is worth taking."

She stared at me a moment before shaking her head. "That's deep. I like it. I'll add it to my mental list of advice."

"Like stop, drop and roll?"

She nodded. "Exactly."

I wondered when that advice might accidentally pop out. Like maybe when fleeing a building during a fire and starting toward the nearest exit? *Not every opportunity is worth taking.*

I mentally shook my head.

After a moment of silence, Skittles finally said, "I'll go get you that file."

"I appreciate that."

As she skipped away, I opened the door to my office and stepped inside. The first thing I noticed was a paper on my desk.

I stepped closer and looked at the words scribbled across the white sheet.

You don't belong here. Leave!

My blood went cold.

Someone had gotten inside my office and left this. But who?

The first person who came to my mind was . . . Heather's killer.

CHAPTER TEN

AN HOUR LATER, Joseph had left to pick up Heather's parents at the airport. I didn't envy the task before him. I'd offered to join him, but he'd insisted on doing it himself.

As soon as they arrived at the school, I planned on finding them to offer my condolences.

Right now, I stared at a copy of the file Skittles had brought me. I'd asked her to make a copy of the contents for me and return the original so no one would notice it was missing. Then I thanked her, gave her a list of tasks for the day, and politely asked if she'd shut the door on her way out.

She did.

As soon as I had a moment to myself, I opened the folder and scanned Heather's details.

Why was I doing this?

Because someone had killed my old friend's daughter and was now desperately scrambling to cover up the crime. I wanted to call the police and ask them if the autopsy report was back yet.

But I didn't. I knew they probably wouldn't tell me anyway.

However, the mysterious incidents surrounding participants in the talent show—the front-runners, from what I understood—indicated there was more going on than met the eye.

I wanted to figure out why.

Was I doing this simply because I loved my job and wanted to excel at it?

That's what I told myself. My job was to put out fires, and it was hard to put out a fire if you didn't know why it had ignited in the first place. But another part of me was simply concerned for my former college roommate upon the loss of her daughter.

I knew all about loss. I knew how gut-wrenching it could be. How all-consuming.

Even though I knew the police were working on this and that I should simply let them do their jobs, that didn't mean I couldn't do a little digging myself. If there was one thing the men in my life had taught me, it was the art of deconstructing a crime.

My father had been an expert.

Mostly because he was a criminal.

Besides, doing PR work was a lot like solving a crime. I had to piece things together for a happy outcome. Sometimes, that piecing together took on different forms.

Like unraveling a mystery.

I studied Heather's information. Much of it was basic.

Heather was twenty years old. An A student. No disciplinary action had ever been taken against her. She'd been a RA in her resident hall, a member of Alpha Beta Sorority, and she worked three days a week in the college cafeteria.

I paused at her medical history, staring at the notation about her severe peanut allergy.

What if . . . I could be totally off base here . . . but what if someone had put peanut dust on that microphone cover before Heather sang? And what if that act had been caught on video? Only the person who'd done it hadn't realized the camera was on at the time?

Certainly, the police had taken that microphone so they could check it.

I heard a footstep outside my room and quickly closed the folder, slipping it into a desk drawer before the wrong person saw me with it. That was also the same place I'd stashed the threatening note I'd received.

I hadn't told anyone about it yet. The threat didn't seem like something I should report to the police, though I was considering it. I needed more time to think it through first.

Phil would have told me I should. But Phil and I hadn't always seen eye to eye on everything either.

A moment later, someone knocked on my door, and I called for them to come in.

Detective Garrison stepped inside wearing some dark wash jeans and a long-sleeved gray shirt that looked designer with its washed-out edges. His hair was still wet, making me think he'd just showered and come right here.

He nodded at me. "Mrs. Paine. Do you have a moment?"

I wondered why he was coming to see me. I had no reason to feel nervous, but I did.

"Yes, of course." I nodded to the mid-century-style leather seat across from me. "Please, make yourself comfortable. Would you like some water?"

I had some bottles stashed in the cabinet behind me. I'd sent Professor Skittles to get them for me this morning so I could have some on hand for occasions such as this.

He sat stiffly in the chair, his large frame overpowering the small piece. "No, I'm afraid I don't have that kind of time. I wanted to thank you for your help last night."

He was thanking me now? That was a change, considering the fact that he'd seemed irritated with me last night.

I kept those thoughts to myself.

"Of course. Have there been any developments that you're able to tell me about?" I held my breath, hoping that might be the case.

He pressed his lips together in what almost appeared to be a grimace. "I wish I had more. But we *do* have a preliminary cause of death."

I held my breath again, anxious to know if my theory was correct. "Heather died of anaphylactic shock, didn't she?"

He flinched as he seemed to register surprise. "How did you know?"

I shrugged and shifted in my office chair. "Good guess, I suppose."

"Like I said, it's only a preliminary result, but we found peanut dust on the microphone cover."

"Who put it there?" I blurted.

The wrinkle between his eyes deepened. "We don't believe anyone *put it there*. Not on purpose, at least. Like I said last night, Heather's death isn't being treated as a murder or foul play."

I frowned. The matter seemed so clear to me. Peanut dust when combined with a prestigious competition and a missing camera equaled high stakes.

"How can it be anything but foul play?" I asked.

Garrison swallowed hard enough that I heard the saliva swishing in his mouth.

He was nervous, I realized.

But why?

"If you must know, the singer who warmed up before Heather had just eaten some peanuts," Garrison finally said. "Some residue must have been left on the microphone cover. The other student feels terrible about it, of course. But it was a tragic accident. That's all."

Despite his nerves, Garrison seemed a little too confident—or maybe he was too stubborn or arrogant—for my comfort. That explanation didn't answer all my questions. "What about the stolen camera? And my purse?"

His lips twitched. "We're still trying to figure those things out. But the incidents could be unrelated. I know that seems coincidental, but sometimes in investigations there *are* coincidences."

I still wasn't buying it. "If that's true, then why are you looking so hard for whoever stole the camera?"

He narrowed his eyes. "Just to cover all our bases."

I swallowed back my argument. I wouldn't fight with the detective. After all, he had more experience than I did.

In theory.

If he was correct, that would be good news for the school.

But Garrison was wrong. I had no doubt about that.

"What am I allowed to release to the public?" I finally asked, snapping back into professional demeanor.

"Nothing yet. No names. Not until we meet with Heather's parents."

"Understood."

But, as Garrison left, all I could think about was

something my father used to say. *Every great criminal is a master at concealing the truth.*

So who was this criminal who'd so effortlessly covered up this crime by sprinkling doubt in people's minds?

AFTER GARRISON LEFT, I glanced at my watch. Based on a quick estimation, I figured I still had at least an hour before Joseph would arrive with Heather's parents. In the meantime, I headed to Hannon Auditorium.

I stepped into the space and saw I wasn't the only one there. Apparently, the scene had been cleared and now some of the tech crew was working onstage.

My gaze stopped on the man sitting behind the soundboard.

Devin Pearson. We weren't students here together, but he was widely regarded as one of the best sound techs in the business. He'd worked some of my concerts back in the day.

I climbed the steps so I could meet him at the sound booth. His eyes lit with recognition when he saw me.

"If it isn't Camryn Paine. I heard you were back,

but now that I'm seeing it with my own eyes, I still find it hard to believe."

I grinned when I heard the enthusiasm in his voice. "Good to see you too, Devin."

He was a large, imposing black man with a deep voice. I'd guess him to be in his early fifties, although he'd aged well. Really well. No wrinkles or any other of the normal signs of aging. The fact he kept himself physically fit helped.

I'd always liked Devin, with his outgoing personality and wide smile. Plus, he really knew music and was a genius at mixing a sound board.

"What's this I hear about you wasting your talents by doing PR? Girl, you were meant to be up there onstage." He pulled a lip back and stared at me like I'd just told him a lie.

I shrugged. This wasn't the first time I'd had to address this question. "We all have different chapters in our life. This is mine for now."

"Well, you have to follow your heart." He leaned back and crossed his thick arms over his chest. "What can I do for you? I assume you didn't come here so we could reminisce about old concerts together."

I lowered myself into one of the chairs beside

him. I wished that was the case, but unfortunately, it wasn't.

I rubbed my lips together before starting. "I'm sure you're aware of what happened yesterday."

He frowned and nodded. "I wasn't in here myself. I had a doctor's appointment. But I left one of my students in charge."

"I'm curious. The police say that peanut dust was left on the microphone cover and that's why Heather died."

Devin clucked his tongue and shook his head. "That's terrible."

"I know. I'm just curious about your process with the equipment. When was that microphone put out and how often do you change the microphone covers?"

He let out a long breath and stared at the stage. "I put the microphones out myself yesterday morning before I left for my appointment. And the microphone covers remain on for each act. We don't change them out, and I don't think any students make an effort to do that themselves, even though they would be more than welcome to."

"But what you set up onstage doesn't remain there for the entire performance because there are different kinds of acts, correct? Some groups might be a quartet while others might be solos and such."

"That's right, but it's not like we have dance numbers or anything here. So we usually have six mics for singing groups and choir mics for the larger groups."

"But all the equipment you used yesterday was already there and it was already set up?"

"That's right." He studied me for a minute. "Why are you asking?"

"I'm just curious. There's something about what happened that rubs me the wrong way."

I didn't want to go around telling everybody that I was looking deeper into this. I knew better than to do that. At least, I liked to *think* I knew better. That reminder was only compounded when I remembered the threatening note I'd received.

"If you're thinking someone put the peanut dust there, I find it hard to believe. Heather was only the fifth act to warm up yesterday. There were four before her. Otherwise, it was just the stagehands who would have had access."

I scanned the dark stage. "How many stagehands do you have?"

He rubbed his chin. "We had about four or five working yesterday."

My mind continued to calculate what might have happened. "Are any of them working now?"

He nodded to the stage as a student wearing all black ran a dustmop across the shiny wood floor. "Langston was working yesterday. Would you like to talk to him?"

He sounded like just the person I wanted to talk to. "As a matter of fact, I would."

He grabbed a mic, hit a switch, and then put the device to his mouth. "Langston, can you come up here?"

Langston froze and looked up at the balcony, where Devin addressed him.

"Is everything okay?" the boy called.

"I just want to talk to you about a couple of things."

Langston squinted up at us, blinded by the stage lights. "Do you mind if I ask what it's about?"

Devin frowned, clearly annoyed by the fact his student was questioning him. "It doesn't matter what it's about. I asked you to come up here to talk. Now you're just wasting my time."

Langston stared another moment before nodding. He lowered the dustmop onto the floor and started toward the steps leading from the stage.

But instead of heading toward them, he

suddenly turned on his heel and dashed behind the curtains instead.

My breath caught.

Had he just run away?

People usually ran for one reason . . . guilt.

CHAPTER ELEVEN

"WHAT IN THE WORLD?" Devin muttered as he jumped to his feet and stared after Langston.

"Looks like he might be hiding something." I frowned.

"I'd say we should go after him, but by the time we get down the steps, he'll be long gone." Devin shook his head as he sat back down and leaned back in his seat. He pressed his lips together in disappointment.

My thoughts continued to turn over in my mind, and excitement zinged through me—excitement because this seemed like a potential lead.

"What's Langston like?" I asked.

Devin pressed his lips together again before

grunting. "He's a little strange. A little jumpy. But I can't see him hurting anyone."

"What do you mean by strange?" There could be a lot of potential definitions to go with that word.

Devin shrugged and stared at the stage as if deep in thought. "He's quirky. A loner. One of the best drummers I've ever heard. He transforms into a different person when he's onstage. And as soon as he's finished performing, he turns into a mouse again."

"He must be a freshman." Freshmen were usually assigned as stagehands so they could learn the ins and outs of the business. Students at Grand Isle earned the right to be onstage.

"That's right. He lives on campus, and I don't think he has a car, so he couldn't have gotten but so far."

I nodded. "Good to know because I'm going to want to talk to him and figure out what that was about."

Devin rubbed his jaw and nodded. "You're not the only one."

My phone buzzed, and I glanced down to see a message from Joseph saying that he was done meeting with Heather's parents.

"I've got to run," I told Devin. "But it's really good to see you."

"Same here."

I hurried from the auditorium, glancing around as I did. I wanted to make sure Langston wasn't anywhere lurking. I didn't think that he was, but I wanted to be certain—especially since someone seemed to feel threatened by me.

It was the only reason they would have left that note on my desk.

I didn't see Langston anywhere around.

What a strange reaction. What exactly was the boy hiding?

I was going to have to wait a little longer to find out.

Instead, I hurried back to the admin building. As soon as I walked into the senior leadership wing, I spotted Joseph talking with Rebecca and Ned in the lobby area outside his office.

When Rebecca saw me, her shoulders slumped and a cry escaped. "Camryn . . ."

I quickly closed the space between us and pulled her into my arms. "I'm so sorry, Rebecca."

Rebecca had always been such a kind, melancholy soul. She felt things deeply and loved deeply.

She sniffled before another sob escaped. "I just can't believe this."

"I can't either. We're all in shock, but I can't even imagine what you're going through."

She pulled away from our embrace and wiped beneath her eyes using a crumpled tissue. "It just seems surreal. I keep expecting I'll wake up and realize this was all just a nightmare. But that's not going to happen, is it?"

As she began sobbing again, Ned pulled her into his arms.

A sickly feeling formed in my stomach. I wished I could take away their pain. To bring Heather back. To promise them that things would get easier. But that was impossible.

"We're about to go to the police station." Rebecca's breath caught, but she swallowed and seemed to pull herself together for another moment. "I heard about the candlelight vigil tonight. We'll stay for that and maybe another day to collect the things from her room. I don't know. Everything just feels so wrong right now."

"We're here for you whatever you need. Would you like me to go with you?"

Rebecca shook her head, an empty, shellshocked look in her gaze. "No, we can handle it, but thank you."

My resolve was even stronger now than it was before.

Whoever had done this to Heather needed to be brought to justice.

———

I KNEW Heather's parents wanted to go to her dorm and collect her things later. Before they did, I wanted to look at her room.

I headed toward her residence hall, smiling and calling hello to everyone I passed.

Public relations didn't just mean how I represented the school to the outside world. It was important to build a good rapport within the organization too.

This was what I'd learned from a decade of working in the field.

My mentor had said I was a natural. I didn't know about that, but I did know I found the work fulfilling. I liked putting out fires, especially for a cause I believed in. I was picky about the work I did, and I refused to work for just any business that asked me.

As soon as I walked into Tybee Hall, memories flooded me. My room had been on the second floor of this dormitory. I'd spent many late nights there making music, laughing, and talking about boys.

Talking about *Weston*.

I frowned. That seemed like another lifetime ago.

I set those thoughts aside as I went to the third floor to Room 312. I wasn't sure if Heather's roommate would be here, but I hoped she was. Classes had been canceled today so students could deal with Heather's untimely death.

I'd looked up her roommate's name before leaving. Willow Snyder. She was a junior. In the classical academy. A soprano.

I knocked.

Voices drifted from the other side of the door, and I knew at least two people were inside.

But there was no answer.

I knocked again and finally heard soft footsteps. The door opened just a crack and a girl with red-rimmed eyes stared at me. "Can I help you?"

"I hope so," I started. "I'm Camryn Paine, and I'm—"

The door opened wider. "You were that singer . . . my mom and dad used to listen to you."

"Is that right?" I felt so old when people said things like that.

"My dad said you had the voice of an angel."

I smiled. The truth was, I never quite knew how to respond to those comments, even after all these years.

Instead, I changed the subject. "Are you Heather's roommate, Willow?"

Her face instantly sobered, all her excitement from meeting me disappearing and grief taking its place. "Yes . . . well, I was her roommate. I still can't believe I have to say that in past tense."

She drew in a shaky breath, and I thought for a moment she might burst into tears.

My heart softened with compassion, and the motherly part of me wanted to pull the girl into my arms. But I didn't. That would be too weird.

Instead, I said, "I'm sorry for your loss. I know this is probably a bad time, but I wondered if we could talk?"

Her face tensed as if unpleasant possibilities rushed through her mind until she finally nodded. "Of course. Anything for Heather."

As she led me into the room, the other student inside rose and said she'd come back later. That was fine by me. Some privacy might actually be good.

I glanced around the space, surprised that the basics looked similar to when I'd been a student. A common living area was situated in the center of the room, with a door on either side, each leading to a bedroom. At the back of the space was a shared bathroom.

Heather and Willow had decorated their living space in bold colors with a black-and-white chevron rug in the center. A mirror with a fuchsia frame hung on the wall, a bright yellow planter sat by the window, and two lime-green chairs stood in the corner.

The whole place smelled like cheerful flowers, probably from the small infuser of fragrant oil plugged into a wall near the door.

Willow and I sat on a small couch draped with a white shabby-chic slipcover, and I turned toward Willow. "I was wondering if you could tell me a little bit more about Heather."

She stared at me. "Why? Is this for the candle-light vigil tonight?"

"Partly, yes," I said. "But I'd also like to learn more about Heather because I want to make sure I do right by her."

"The police are saying it was a freak accident, but some of the students think someone might have done this to Heather on purpose. Is that true?" Willow's voice cracked as she stared at me with wide eyes that almost appeared afraid of whatever answer I might give.

"The police are still looking into things." I knew I couldn't say too much. "If they learn anything, I'm sure that we will let the student body know."

Willow nodded, her gaze both hollow and fidgety at the same time. "What do you want to know?"

I glanced at the shelf beside me and saw a picture of Heather and Willow in a thick black frame. A live oak tree with moss draped on its branches stood behind them, the sun peeking between branches. The smiles on their faces were full of promise.

Certainly, neither of them had anticipated this turn of events.

Grief was like that.

My throat burned as I turned back to Willow. "How did Heather seem lately? I noticed when she was warming up yesterday, her voice was a little pitchy. But I also know that can't be normal. Not if she was accepted here at Grand Isle."

Grand Isle got hundreds of applicants every year, and only 5 percent of those who applied were accepted. To get into the school you had to be an exceptional musician and full of potential.

Willow frowned and picked up the ukulele resting on a wall hanger beside the couch. She began to absently pluck the strings in a sad little ditty. "She wasn't exactly acting like herself lately."

"Do you know why?"

"She didn't really talk to me about it, but she did seem preoccupied. I was a little worried about her." She plucked a few more strings.

"Maybe she didn't talk to you about it, but do you have any guesses about what was wrong? Just between you and me."

Willow rested her hands on the neck board of the ukulele and glanced around as if unsure if she wanted to say anything. Then she leaned closer. "I know she was stressed over finances."

"Finances as far as paying for school?" Maybe I was onto something.

"Yes, I think so."

"But isn't her mom part of a symphony out on the West Coast?" That was the last I'd heard.

"She was until rheumatoid arthritis kicked in about three years ago—right before Heather came here. Now her mom can't play the violin anymore.

Her dad worked in finance, but he got laid off from his job six months ago."

"That's terrible." I hadn't heard that. I really should have kept up with Rebecca more.

"Heather had a couple of scholarships, but not enough to pay her whole way."

"I understand. And if she can't pay . . . ?"

Willow frowned. "Then she would have to leave. She had way too much talent to do that."

Heather's dilemma caused unrest to jostle inside me. "So, what was she going to do?"

Willow shrugged and hugged the ukulele to her chest as if it were a teddy bear. "I'm not sure. She said she had an idea, though."

"When was that?"

"A month or so ago. She seemed to perk up for a while after that."

"But you have no idea why?" The first things that came to my mind were drugs or something else illegal. That was only because my brother told me that's usually where the money could be found.

Joel was a former detective and a great sounding board. I'd call him now except he was working a private security case in Costa Rica.

Willow shook her head. "I know she said she

talked to Weston—Professor Turner, I mean—about it. Whatever he told her seemed to do the trick."

I stored that information away. "Thank you for sharing."

"Of course. Anything I can do to help."

"Were there any men in her life?"

Willow frowned. "Not really."

I glanced around the deceitfully cheerful room —one now marred with tragedy. "Do you mind if I look through Heather's things? I want to get a better feel for what she was like. Her style. Her personality."

"If that's what you need to do . . . I'm going to go across the hall and talk to my friends if that's okay." She set the ukulele back onto the wall hanger.

That was more than okay. That was perfect.

I thanked Willow for her time and waited until she left.

Now, I wanted to find some answers.

CHAPTER TWELVE

I GLANCED around Heather's room, wondering where to start. I knew I didn't have much time, so I should probably go with the most obvious thing: her dresser.

I searched through her drawers.

Nothing.

I searched through her desk.

Also, nothing.

I glanced in her closet.

Again, nothing of interest.

Where else might a girl like Heather hide her secrets?

My eyes stopped on the jewelry box near her bed. Carefully, I walked toward it and lowered myself on the edge of her fuchsia-covered mattress. I picked up the oak box and opened the top.

A song began playing.

"The Music of the Night" from *Phantom of the Opera*.

That was Scarlett's favorite too.

Mostly costume jewelry lay on the top tray. The two drawers beneath it contained the same.

I paused and listened to the haunting strands as they drifted through the room.

There was a catch in the song, like something was blocking the metal cylinder that brushed against the steel comb creating the music.

I squinted to better examine it, wondering what was wrong.

I nibbled on my bottom lip a moment before tugging on the bottom of the top tray. I didn't want to break the box, especially not if it was important to Heather's family. And my hunch could be nothing. I knew that.

Despite that, I kept going.

I needed something to pry beneath it. I found a nail file and slid it between the sides and bottom. A moment later, the tray lifted, revealing a compartment underneath.

My heart pounded harder.

An envelope lay there.

Carefully, I pulled it out and held my breath as I opened it.

I exhaled when I saw the contents.

It was filled with cash.

I quickly counted it.

Two thousand dollars.

Where exactly had Heather gotten this money? Willow had said her roommate was strapped for cash.

A bad feeling brewed in my gut.

Did this stash somehow tie in with Heather's death?

And why hadn't the police found this? Had they even checked out her room or had they simply assumed her death was accidental and closed the case without exploring every possibility?

MY PHONE RANG, pulling me from my thoughts.

Quickly, I put the money back where I'd found it.

Then I glanced at the screen. Joseph was calling me.

I quickly composed myself before answering the video chat. "Hello, Joseph."

His panicked voice practically assaulted my ear. "Somehow reporters got wind of what happened. They've been calling me and asking questions. This isn't good."

I'd figured it was just a matter of time before the media put together the facts that there could be a juicy story here. "Direct them to me, and I'll handle them. This is what you're paying me to do."

"Detective Garrison said this was just a freak accident." Joseph took a long sip of water. "But I know how the media is going to try to paint this."

"Like I said, it's my job to handle this. You just keep your cool, okay?"

His expression froze a moment as if he considered all his possibilities. Finally, he nodded. "Okay. I'll send you all the contact information right now. I won't be able to concentrate until I do."

I ended the call and slipped the phone back into my pocket. Then I glanced around Heather's room one more time to make sure I hadn't missed anything.

I desperately wanted to find out where she'd gotten this money. Heather definitely had some type of side business going on.

I wondered if Weston—Professor Turner—had

any insight on that. Willow had indicated that he might.

My gut twisted at the thought. I didn't want to think that my old boyfriend might have some type of involvement in this, but between his secret conversation with Detective Garrison yesterday and his connection with Heather, it was looking more and more like that all the time.

I slipped out of Heather's room and closed the door behind me.

As I did, the sound of someone singing captured my ear.

The song sounded like "His Eye Is on the Sparrow." But instead of saying, "I sing because I'm happy," the person crooned, "I *clean* because I'm happy."

When I rounded the corner, I spotted a familiar face mopping the hallway floor.

Anita.

The woman took her earbuds out and offered a sheepish grin. "Sorry. Singing is the only thing that gets me through."

"You have a nice voice."

She waved me off. "Oh, stop. You're just being sweet."

"No, you really do. Your tone is very pleasant and easy to listen to."

"You just made my day." Her grin faltered. "What brings you out this way?"

"I'm planning a candlelight vigil for Heather."

Anita leaned against the mop and frowned. "I just can't stop thinking about what happened. It's so tragic."

"It's more than tragic." I observed the woman a moment. "Did you know Heather?"

Anita shrugged. "I wouldn't say I knew her. But I try to talk to the girls on the floor. I feel like they could use a motherly figure, you know?"

"Did you notice anything strange about Heather lately?"

She wrinkled her lips together in thought. "Now that you mention it, I did see a boy come to her room a couple of times."

"To see Heather or her roommate?"

"I can't say for sure, but Heather is the one who greeted him at the door."

My breath caught. "Could you tell me what he looks like?"

"He . . . he wasn't the type I expected to see her with. He was kind of dirty. His hair was blond and messy. He had those holes in his ears. What are they called again? Gorges . . . ?"

"Gauges?"

She snapped her fingers. "Yes, that's it. Gauges. I guess you could say he was rough around the edges."

"How many times did you see them together?"

Anita shrugged. "Maybe twice."

"You ever see this guy before? Is he a student?"

"I don't think so, but I could be wrong." She shrugged again. "Sorry. I wish I could help more."

"No, you were a big help. Thank you."

I needed to figure out how to find this guy. Maybe he had some of the answers I needed.

* * *

I HURRIED BACK across campus to my office. As I did, I still mulled over both Willow's and Anita's words.

Heather had been acting strangely. She had a side business. She had a wad of cash hidden in her room. And a boy had secretly been visiting her—a boy who was unrefined.

Maybe my theory was right. Maybe Heather had found a nice side job selling drugs or something else shady. That would explain why she'd been acting on edge lately.

I didn't want to believe that theory was true. But it made the most sense.

But how was I going to prove that? How was I going to find Gauge Boy?

I didn't know. I would need to think about that one a bit more.

On the short walk from Tybee Hall to the admin building, I saw a news van pulling up outside.

How had word about Heather's death leaked? I suppose the media could have overheard what happened by listening on their scanners. A faculty member or student could have called them.

But if Heather's death was simply an accident, there would be no need for this media fanfare.

Except the media always liked to see the mighty fall.

And the Grand Isle Conservatory of Music was definitely among the mighty. Especially considering all the famous and accomplished people who'd come from this place. Major composers. Record producers. Singers.

I knew one thing for sure. I could handle this. It was what I did.

Now I just needed to turn on the professional side of my personality.

Kind of like my dad used to do. Maybe I'd learned the skills from him.

Because my dad was one of the world's greatest con men. He was in jail now for what he'd done.

I couldn't help but think that maybe I picked up on a few tricks of the trade while growing up around his double life.

CHAPTER THIRTEEN

TWO HOURS LATER, I was back in my office after a successful press conference. I'd been open and honest with them about what had happened, and I assured the media that students were our first priority. I mentioned the grief counselors that had been brought in as well as an email I'd sent out about self-care.

When I'd gotten back, the first thing I'd done was to work with Skittles and the Student Relations Liaison on the candlelight vigil. I thought I had everything in place, and a text message had gone out to all the students about the event.

Afterward, as I sat at my desk snacking, I thought about my next step in figuring out what really happened to Heather. Should I talk to the other front-runners in the competition? Look for Stage-hand Langston? Or try to locate Gauge Boy?

Even more—how did I figure out where Heather had gotten that wad of cash?

Slow down, Camryn.

I swallowed hard as the directive echoed in my head, almost as if Phil himself were reaching down to me from heaven.

What *was* I doing?

The answer was clear. I was jumping in with both feet as if I were an expert. I clearly had no experience in investigating murders. In fact, maybe I'd jumped in too quickly.

Then I remembered the threat I'd received. It seemed like I was already in this pretty deep. Whether I liked it or not, I had to find answers at this point.

Someone lightly knocked on the door. I looked up and saw Weston leaning against the frame. How long had he been standing there?

My heart let out an involuntary flutter at the sight of him.

Not because I was attracted to him—but because I suspected he knew more than he'd let on. That's what I told myself, at least.

"Can I come in?" He straightened, the sparkle in his gaze trying to captivate me.

I wouldn't let it. "Of course."

He stepped inside, a playful smile tugging at his lips. The smile that was always there. That could be read all kinds of ways. The man was both charismatic and tender at the same time.

That very combination had made so many women fall in love with him.

Including me.

He swaggered into my office and, without invitation, lowered himself into the chair across from me. Then he nodded at the desk. "You still eat carrots with mustard?"

I glanced at my desk where I'd been munching on baby carrots dipped in mustard. It was the best snack ever, and I didn't care what anybody else had to say about it.

"It's so tasty. And healthy. You should try it sometime." I held out a carrot, offering him the chance to try.

I'd begun eating the snack when I was on the road touring and had to watch my figure. But I'd liked it so much that I continued to eat it to this day. It had the crunch factor that my stress levels craved.

"No, thank you." He leaned back and crossed an

ankle over his knee. "How are you doing? I saw your press conference. You were a natural, like always."

"I certainly didn't expect to be thrust into this, but thank you."

"You've handled it with grace."

I dipped another carrot into my blob of mustard, my thoughts still revolving around Heather. "Do you know a student named Langston?"

"Langston Murphy?" Surprise registered in Weston's gaze. "Yeah, I know Langston. Why do you ask?"

"Devin tried to ask him some questions about what happened yesterday, and the boy ran away."

A knot formed between Weston's eyes. "Really? That surprises me. Langston can play a mean drum solo. But I know he often seems anxious also."

I studied Weston, trying to decide how much I should reveal next. "I guess you heard confirmation that the police don't think Heather's death was a murder . . ."

Weston flinched, the action so subtle that most people wouldn't have noticed. "That was the impression I had. That's good news, right?"

I watched Weston. More like, I listened to him. I tried to hear any anomalies in his voice. Or in the way his breath caught.

The other thing that I happen to be fairly good at doing was acting as a human lie detector.

I never told anybody that. Because who would want to talk to me if they thought I was always judging them for whether or not they told me the truth?

But I heard things other people didn't. I heard when a person's voice tensed. I heard when their pitch cracked or wavered. When saliva moved inside their mouths as they formulated lies. When they gritted their teeth. Sometimes the signs were very, very subtle.

But I heard those details. I couldn't turn them off.

"Wait." Weston stared at me a moment before twisting his head as if he'd just been thrown a curve ball. "You still don't believe it was a freak accident?"

I didn't say anything, only shrugged. "The freak accident doesn't explain why the lights went out and somebody took that camera."

Slowly, Weston's neck seemed to loosen, and he nodded. "You're right, it doesn't. But that doesn't mean there isn't another explanation for what happened. I mean, think about it. If this was a murder—and that's a big *if*—why would somebody risk exposing themselves like that? If they planted peanut dust on the microphone cover, why come back to witness Heather die? It's too risky. It doesn't make sense."

He still hadn't convinced me. "Like I said, unless there was something on the tape that they realized would implicate them."

He shrugged and tilted his head in thought. "Maybe. But nefarious intentions aren't hiding around every corner."

I sucked on my cheek for a minute. Weston knew about my history. He'd been there when I discovered that my father had a double life. Actually, a quadruple life. Weston knew it was hard for me to accept statements at face value and that I'd learned things often weren't as they seemed.

I wasn't done asking him questions either. I tried to keep my voice soft before I posed my next inquiry. "How well did you know Heather?"

There it was. His breath caught. Just barely. But it was there. And his eyes widened for just a split second in surprise.

He shifted in his seat, no longer looking as laid-back as he had earlier. "She was one of my students. Why are you asking?"

"I'm just trying to find out more information on her."

"So you can figure out if she was murdered?" He narrowed his eyes in disapproval.

"That and because we're planning a candlelight vigil for her tonight. I'd like to gather all the information I can. I just wondered if you knew her. If you ever talked to her outside of class."

I didn't see Weston as the type who'd do anything shady with a student, like having an affair with one of them or something. Then again, he'd always liked pretty women.

It had been just one of many reasons why we'd broken up.

"Heather was a good girl. It's a huge loss for this community that she's gone." Weston slowly rose to his feet. "You might want to consider the fact that you're looking into this a little too hard, almost as if you're looking for something that's not there."

I heard the warning in his voice. His tone had hardened right along with his gaze.

But even as it hardened, tension threaded in his tones—a tension that I couldn't miss.

I couldn't hear his heartbeat—I wasn't *that* good. But I was nearly certain by the sweat across his forehead that his heart was beating harder and faster right now.

"I understand." I knew I couldn't push this anymore. Not for now, at least.

Part of finding answers meant knowing when to push and when to back off. It was something a lot of people got wrong. Phil had taught me that.

"I need to go." Weston stepped toward the door. "But good luck in your new position."

I nodded as I watched him walk away.

What was Weston Turner hiding? I felt certain there was something.

THAT EVENING as the sun began to set, I left my office and joined the rest of the student body and staff on the Cobblestone Lawn.

Cobblestone Lawn was located in the center of the campus, between all the various buildings. True to its name, stones stretched across the area in a Celtic cross pattern. Benches were set up along the perimeter, and lush green grass and trees that were as old as the city itself edged the space.

A stage had been set up in the middle of the area, and a screen stretched taut at the back of the platform. A picture of Heather faded as a new one appeared. Students held candles and took turns talking about their favorite memories of her. In the distance, I saw Joseph standing with Heather's parents as they mourned.

They weren't the only ones crying. Heather had clearly been loved by her classmates.

I stood on the periphery of the group, as always, and I watched. Since I'd just arrived at the school, I didn't feel right being onstage for this event. Instead, the Student Relations Liaison served as emcee instead.

The student behind the mic onstage introduced herself as Megan Howell, one of Heather's best friends. Megan was a brunette with long, wavy hair and oversized glasses. She was petite and dressed in a camisole and cardigan. I'd guess, based purely on her appearance, that she was a part of the classical music program here at the school.

It wasn't that I wanted to stereotype, but oftentimes it was easy to guess which program students were in just by looking at the way they presented themselves.

The classical students always seemed preppy and conservative. The contemporary students—which covered pop, country, and rock—dressed in either trendy clothing, cowboy boots, or had an edgy look. The soul and hip-hop sector usually had a swagger and an urban vibe.

All in all, it was fascinating to see these different groups of people who all loved music but who each approached the art of music from different angles. Sometimes there was friction between the academies because of the different ways students viewed their art.

But, at times like this, everyone pulled together.

As soon as Megan finished speaking, I watched as she joined the rest of the crowd. I wanted to talk to her, but I was going to have to do this carefully so I didn't come across as insensitive.

Before I could thread through the crowd, I saw Rebecca and Ned walk onstage. My throat tightened. What would they say?

Clearly, they were upset. What parents wouldn't be? Their eyes were red, their faces pale, their movements stilted.

"Thank you all for coming out to honor our daughter," Rebecca started. "Though this is a terrible tragedy, I know Heather is looking down from heaven and feeling very loved."

Rebecca said more about Heather, each new sentence heartbreaking in its own way.

As she ended, she said, "I know this is Harvest

Week at the school, and Heather wouldn't want things to shut down because of her death. I want you to know that you have our blessing to continue with your festivities. Life must go on even amid mourning."

As a murmur of approval and surprise rippled through the crowd, I glanced at Megan. She was leaving, headed toward what students called Resident Hall Row. It was the area on campus where most of the dormitories were located.

I didn't want to let her get away without asking a few questions first.

With one last glance at Rebecca and Ned onstage, I took off after Megan, catching her just as she reached one of the sidewalks branching from Cobblestone Lawn.

"Megan! Great job up there," I called to her.

She paused and looked at me cautiously before nodding. "Thank you. That was one of the hardest things I've ever had to do."

"I can only imagine. I'm Camryn, by the way. I just started working here at the school."

She nodded, the standoffish look remaining in her gaze. "I heard some of my classmates talking about you."

I didn't even want to know what they were

saying. Were they talking about my past musical career? Or my dad's very public trial for everything he'd done as a con artist? Or maybe my husband's untimely death. There were too many options for me to even think about right now.

"It sounds like you and Heather were really close. I'm sorry for your loss."

Megan wiped underneath her eyes again and stared off in the distance as she tried to compose herself. "We were. I still can't believe she's gone. I can't believe that something as simple as someone eating peanuts was the cause."

"It sounded like Heather had a very severe allergy."

"She did. She carried that EpiPen everywhere. But this happened so fast. Her purse was behind stage. I'm sure she didn't even know what was going on."

I shifted. "I heard Heather was having some financial trouble here at the school. Is that true?"

Disbelief flooded her gaze. "I'm surprised you heard about that. But, yes, Heather was pretty stressed out about money for a while. Then she found a way to make some additional cash, and that really helped her feel better."

I licked my lips before asking my next question. "Do you know exactly what that way was?"

Megan shrugged. "I'm not sure. I know she was creating something, and she couldn't do it in the dormitory. She found another place to use, though."

My first thought was meth. But where would Heather make meth here on campus?

Maybe meth seemed too extreme, but my brother said desperate people figured out how to make the drug and then sold it for a lot of money. It was especially prevalent at some colleges.

"Do you have any idea where she went to do this?" I asked.

"Not really." Megan started to shrug when she froze. "Well, on second thought . . . maybe. One time I saw her walking to the maintenance building on campus. When I asked her about it, she got all weird."

My breath caught. "Really?"

"I don't know if that has anything to do with her side business or not, but . . . I don't know why else she would be headed there."

"Was she dating anyone?" I remembered the blond Anita had mentioned.

Megan shrugged. "I think she had a crush on

some guy, but she wasn't officially dating. She would have told me if she was."

As one of the vocal groups at the school started singing a Pentatonix-like version of "Hallelujah," I glanced across the lawn and spotted Weston. A pretty, twenty-something brunette flounced up to him and planted a kiss on his cheek. He grinned down at her before pulling her into a hug.

I recoiled at the sight of it.

Was that his girlfriend? A twenty-something who was young enough to have been his student at one time? Part of me wasn't surprised.

I turned back to Megan. "Thank you for your help. And, again, I'm really sorry for your loss."

"Thank you." With a wave, Megan walked away.

I needed to check out the maintenance building. I wanted to see if I could figure out what Heather was doing there.

Maybe now was as good a time as any.

CHAPTER FOURTEEN

I STARTED toward the maintenance building when I heard murmuring in the crowd behind me.

I pivoted toward the sound. The multitude split as if parting for a guest of honor.

What exactly was going on here?

Then I spotted him.

Oden McIntyre.

He was a maker of stars, in a close running with Simon Cowell. He knew how to pick out talent and make people into cultural icons.

He was the one who'd plucked me out of obscurity.

And he hadn't spoken to me since I walked away from it all.

What was he doing at Grand Isle?

I watched as people stared at him, their lips parting in awe as if they were stunned to be around such greatness.

My fists clenched in anger. This vigil was supposed to be about Heather.

Why had Oden shown up now and brought attention onto himself?

"He's supposed to be a judge for the talent show."

I glanced over as Jinky appeared beside me. I'd noticed her standing several feet away with some other professors earlier. In my distraction, I hadn't even noticed her coming this way.

I continued staring at the man as he waved to everyone around him before pushing his sunglasses up higher on his nose. His designer clothes looked freshly pressed and his hair newly gelled. He wore his trademark black V-neck T-shirt and jeans, along with a gold chain and earring.

"He knows how to make an entrance," I muttered.

"Talk about terrible timing." Jinky frowned. "I heard he's changed. That he gave up all his money to help children in Africa."

I did a double take at her. "Where did you hear that?"

"Somewhere online."

"You know what they say . . . you can't believe everything you see on the internet." If that was true about Oden, I would have *definitely* heard by now. There was no chance that was what he'd done.

I continued to watch as Oden walked toward Joseph and paused beside him. Oden slipped up the sunglasses and rested them atop his head.

Seeing him caused my stomach to clench.

I didn't like him. I didn't like him *at all*.

If I'd been a stronger person back when I'd first started in the music industry, I would have done a lot of things differently. There was a lot I wouldn't have let Oden get away with.

I felt Jinky's gaze burning into me. "Why do you look like you're staring at your worst enemy right now?"

"Oden's not my favorite person." It wasn't a big secret. Tabloids ran a lot of stories with speculations about me and Oden. Most of that speculation involved the two of us having a secret affair—which hadn't happened.

But I couldn't help but think that Weston might have believed those headlines. Our relationship had been at a turning point then anyway. Had those rumors been the icing on the cake?

I shut the thoughts down. I didn't want to go there right now.

"Are you going to talk to him?" Jinky raised her eyebrows as she waited for my answer.

Did I want to talk to Oden? No.

Should I talk to him? Especially since I was now the CCO here at the school?

Probably yes.

But I wasn't in the mood right now. Besides, he had enough people feeding his ego.

Instead, I wanted to check out the maintenance building.

What better time than now while everyone was distracted?

I'D MADE it only halfway down the sidewalk when I heard footsteps behind me.

Heavy footsteps but not too heavy, indicating a person that probably weighed between one-eighty and one-ninety. Based on the gait, this person was athletic. Based on the lack of heavy breathing, he wasn't too old.

Before I even turned around, I knew it was Weston.

"Where are you heading?" He caught up with me and began walking beside me.

I glanced over at him and tried to pretend that my breath didn't catch—especially when I remembered the young woman I'd seen him with. "Just stretching my legs."

"Because of Oden?"

Weston knew all about Oden.

"Oden does not determine any of my actions."

"Understood." Weston nodded, almost as if impressed. "Mind if I walk with you?"

Even though Weston had asked, I wasn't sure if he was *really* asking. I had a feeling he was going to be beside me whether I liked it or not. Besides, maybe it would be good to have him around.

"Not at all," I finally said.

He shifted and drew in a deep breath. "Look, I want to apologize if I got a little snippy with you earlier about what happened with Heather. I'm sorry. I just don't want to see anyone else get hurt."

"I appreciate your concern, but I'm a big girl. I can handle myself."

"I didn't say you couldn't. I just . . ." He seemed like he wanted to say more but finally shook his head. "I just wanted to say I'm sorry."

"Apology accepted."

As we walked, I spotted three girls hurrying away from the candlelight vigil with their heads bent low. One of them peered over her shoulder as if to make sure no one was watching. Another nearly stumbled over a crack in the sidewalk.

They seemed . . . nervous.

But why?

I narrowed my eyes as I watched them. "I wonder why they're leaving."

Weston frowned and rubbed his chin before placing his hands back in his pockets. "Some people just can't handle events like these very well."

"But they look more than sad, don't they? They almost look . . . fearful."

"You drew that conclusion just from watching them walk away?" He raised his eyebrows. "I knew you had supersonic hearing, but it sounds like your powers of observation have only gotten better with time also."

"It's the way their shoulders are hunched. The way they're whispering. It makes them look nervous."

Weston didn't say anything for a moment until he finally nodded. "You're an interesting lady, Camryn Paine."

I stole a glance at him, wondering if there was a

secret insult in his statement. "You're interesting too, Weston Turner."

He smiled before letting out a breath and continuing forward. "So where are you really headed?"

I resisted a sigh. "Toward the maintenance building."

He did a double take at me. "Why would you need to go to the maintenance building?"

"Because I heard that Heather Klein liked to hang out there sometimes, and I find that weird." There was no need to skirt around the truth.

"So . . . you're not dropping this. I'd think you'd want her death to be accidental since it's better PR for the college. Still tragic, don't get me wrong. But it's much better than a murder."

"I understand," I told him. "But something about this whole thing won't let my mind stop working. I'm going to keep looking into this until I feel certain the police came to the correct conclusion."

His eyebrows flickered up as we continued across the campus. "I've got to admire your determination. I've been wanting to ask you—what made you decide to go into PR?"

That time in my life flashed back into my mind, almost as if it were just yesterday. "Phil and I moved into a new neighborhood, and I felt like I'd stepped into the show *Desperate Housewives*. I couldn't believe how catty and gossipy the women were. In my experience, it was partly because they had nothing better to do. Their husbands had high-powered jobs and were gone all the time."

"Ouch."

I shrugged, not apologizing for speaking my truth. "It's just my perspective. Anyway, I didn't want to be one of those superficial women, so I decided I was going to go back to college. At thirty years old, that's what I did. I got my degree in public relations and communications."

"Impressive."

I inhaled a deep breath, wondering if that was a magnolia tree I smelled on the breeze. Whatever the scent, it was lovely . . . as was the smear of pink and purple in the sky as the sun sank.

"I don't know if it was impressive," I said. "But I was much happier getting out of that other situation."

"You've never been the catty type. It was one thing I always liked about you."

"I've always known that if people talk to you about other people, then they will talk to other people about you."

"True that."

We reached the brick-sided maintenance building—built to fit the style of the rest of the campus—and I paused by the metal door. "Do you know anyone who works here?"

"Know them? I can't say I know them. But I've talked to the head of maintenance before. He's a nice guy named Harvey."

Harvey? I remembered meeting him right after Heather died.

I took a deep breath before opening the door and stepping inside. I simply needed to act like I belong here, not like I was snooping. People could smell snoops from a mile away—kind of like I could hear a lie.

I glanced around but didn't see anyone inside. Instead, a large, dark room filled with tools and equipment and lawnmowers stared back.

"Hello?" With Weston by my side, I stepped farther into the space.

No response. But I wasn't ready to give up yet. I heard life in this place.

Toward the back of the building.

It sounded like a saw. Like wood hitting a metal surface. Like a cord rubbing against the floor—maybe from something that had been plugged in.

"Let me guess," Weston muttered. "You're going to go check that sound out?"

"I do like being thorough."

"Yes, you're always very thorough." A touch of amusement tinged his voice.

I hurried toward a door at the back wall. I nudged it, and the wooden door drifted open. As it did, I spotted a man bent over a table saw. Sparks flew. Sawdust fell. Warmth flooded from the small space.

But those things weren't what struck me the most.

What struck me the most was the tall boy with puffy blond hair and gauge earrings.

He fit the description of the boy Anita had said she'd seen Heather hanging out with.

Had I just stumbled upon a lead?

CHAPTER FIFTEEN

I KNOCKED on the door and raised my voice. "Hello!"

The boy didn't hear me.

I knocked again and called louder. "Hello!"

Still no response.

On the third try, the boy turned the saw off just as I raised my voice another decibel.

He startled as he turned toward us.

Weston and I had clearly scared him.

"I didn't hear anyone back there." He tugged his safety goggles to the top of his head and wiped away the sweat there. "Talk about giving a guy a heart attack."

"Sorry, but I *did* call hello a couple of times."

He pulled some plugs from his ears and wiped his brow again.

The scent of freshly cut wood rose around me, along with sweat and the burning scent of the saw as it had spun.

"I can't really hear anything back here." He glanced back and forth between the two of us, a touch of tension pulling through his gaze. "Can I help you?"

"Do you work here in the maintenance department?" I asked.

The boy squirmed as if the question made him uncomfortable. "No. But my father does."

Weston let out a grunt and nodded. "Your father must be Harvey."

Gauge Boy nodded. "I'm Ricky. My dad lets me use the equipment after hours. I guess this place is officially off limits, but as long as I clean up after myself so no one knows I've been here, he's usually fine with it."

"I'm Camryn, and this is Weston," I started. "Are you a student here also?"

He shook his head. "No. I want to go to trade school instead, but I haven't started yet."

"Listen, Ricky," I started. "I have some questions I hope you'll answer for me."

His gaze became even more stilted. "Questions about what?"

"Did you know Heather Klein?" I listened for any hints that he was about to lie to me.

Ricky's breath caught, and he licked his lips. "Maybe. Why?"

"I heard she was hanging out with someone who fits your description and that she liked to slip away to the maintenance building." I stared at him as I waited for his response.

He raised a shoulder defensively before nudging his chin in the air in blatant defiance. "So what if she did? We weren't doing anything wrong."

"We didn't say you were doing anything wrong." Weston's diplomacy seemed to take over. "We're just trying to find out some information. What happened to Heather was tragic. I'm sure you know that better than anyone."

He stared a moment before finally nodding. "Yes, it was."

Weston's charm had worked—of course.

I wasn't complaining.

"Can you tell us the nature of your relationship with Heather?" Weston asked.

Ricky shrugged. "I know how it might look, but we were just friends."

I tilted my head. There was something about the catch in his voice that indicated he wasn't telling the whole truth. "Are you sure about that?"

He rolled his eyes slightly as he tilted his head and let out a sigh. Finally, Ricky let out an even longer breath as if he was about to come clean. "The truth is . . . Heather and I were business partners."

This was it. This was how Heather was making her money.

My heart rate quickened. "What exactly was your business?"

A new emotion flickered through his gaze. "I'd rather not tell you. I can show you instead."

He turned and grabbed something from his tool bench.

As he did, I sucked in a breath.

If he was involved with illegal drugs, then he had a lot at stake. A whole profitable business perhaps.

What if he was grabbing a gun to silence us?

I braced myself.

Because of all the ways I envisioned myself dying, this wasn't it.

INSTEAD OF COMING at us with a weapon, Ricky held up a piece of wall art with various boards arranged vertically across the center.

The wood pieces were all different colors—different stains. But I wasn't sure if there was a deeper meaning behind the design. What was I looking at?

"Did you make this?" I asked.

"I did. It's Heather's idea, and I was just helping her with it. Heather had this idea to do vocal recordings of people saying little phrases—like a kid telling his parents 'I love you' or a groom telling his soon to be bride that she's the best thing that ever happened to him. Heather would record the soundwaves."

"And that's what you created on this board. Soundwaves." I reached forward and touched some of the lines, impressed with Heather's creativity.

"Exactly. Then she printed out the actual soundwave image, as well as a QR code so when people hung the artwork in their house, they could scan the QR code and hear the person's actual voice."

"That's brilliant." Weston's voice trailed with a touch of admiration.

A new wave of sadness filled Ricky's gaze. "I thought so too. She had the creative skills, and I had the woodworking skills, so we made a good team."

"It sounds like you did. Did you have a lot of clients?"

"Heather set the business up online, and we were getting more orders than we could handle. But she said the work allowed her to stay in college and pay her bills. She called it an answer to prayer."

"It sounds like it was." I frowned as I realized Heather's dreams would never be realized. "I hope you figure out a way to continue doing this."

Ricky rubbed beneath his eyes, and I wondered if he was fighting tears. He cared for Heather more than he was letting on. I heard it in his pitch whenever he said her name. His voice became more raspy, airy. His tone more affectionate.

"I'm still trying to figure all that out. But we have some orders we'd already begun working on. I know Heather would want me to finish those."

I took a step back. "We'll let you get back to work. I'm sorry for your loss."

"Thank you."

It looked like I'd just eliminated Heather's income source as a potential reason for murder.

Now I had to look at the next thing on my list and see if I could narrow this down any more.

CHAPTER SIXTEEN

AS I WANDERED from the maintenance building, Weston remained beside me. We walked slowly, which was good since I was lost in my thoughts. Weston didn't seem in a hurry either.

I glanced up at him. I knew him well enough to guess what he was thinking. Even if, at one time in his life, he'd had a big head, he'd still remained chivalrous.

"You're going to walk me home, aren't you?" I murmured.

He shrugged, a twinkle in his gaze as he moseyed beside me. "I thought about it."

I hesitated a moment, wondering if I should release the thought in my head. Finally, I decided not to hold back. It was better to get things out in the open.

"You don't need to feel any obligation to watch out for me just because we have a past together." I kept my voice soft, not wanting to offend him.

"I thought I would try to watch out for you because we're friends."

I glanced at him, a jolt of surprise—and hesitancy—slicing through me. "But are we? I don't say that to sound harsh. I really don't. But I'm also not one to play games. We haven't talked to each other in years, and things didn't exactly end on a good note."

He shrugged and cast a warm glance my way. "But I never felt like we lost touch even though I suppose we did."

"Our lives went in different directions."

He let out a sardonic chuckle. "They really did." His steps slowed as we headed toward the gate at the front of the campus. "But that doesn't mean I didn't think about you and wonder how you were doing. It doesn't mean that I don't care."

A knot formed in my throat when I heard the sincerity in his voice. "I saw that you came to Phil's funeral, and I really did appreciate that."

"You saw me there?" His gaze flickered with surprise.

Memories tried to pummel me, but I held them back. This wasn't the time I wanted to relive those moments. "I did, but you slipped away before I could say anything."

"I didn't know if me being there would make you feel better or upset you. Plus, I was on the road on my farewell tour, and I had to get back. I didn't have much time."

That must have been right before he came here to Grand Isle . . . "I understand. It was nice for you to come. Thank you."

"It's no problem."

We walked a few more steps. Strolled really. That was what you did on cobblestone streets.

Weston rested his hands in his pockets, looking as casual and laid-back as ever as he glanced at me again. "You know, it really is surreal that you're here again, Camryn. Sometimes, I feel like I've stepped back in time."

I chuckled—a rolling, casual sound that quickly faded. I totally understood where he was coming from. "Believe me, I never expected to be here again. When Joseph called and said the conservatory was struggling, I knew I wanted to do something. The school means a lot to me."

"I didn't know if it meant a lot to you or if you

resented it."

"I've gone back and forth between both. But Grand Isle helped make me the person I am today."

We reached the edge of the campus and started down the sidewalk running alongside the cobblestone road to my apartment.

I glanced up at Weston, curiosity burning inside me—despite my resolve to keep my distance. "What about you, Weston? Why are you here and not touring? You have such a huge fan base. People love you."

He shrugged, a new heaviness surrounding him as if my question had stirred up bad memories. "It was just time for a change. For a break. Creatively, I was getting burnt out. It's pretty hard to have any kind of life when you're on the road all the time."

"I know. It is."

We reached the apartment and slowly walked beside each other up the stairs and to my door. Then I turned to him, hating the awkward feeling that fluttered in my stomach. Why did I feel awkward? This was Weston. Sure, the man had once broken my heart, but the past was in the past. We could still be friends.

Back when I'd been in my twenties, finding

someone to spend the rest of my life with was really important. But now I'd been there and done that.

I had a decent life now as a single forty-something woman and didn't feel a pressing need to find someone. If I ever married again, it would only be because I found someone I couldn't imagine living without. He would have to be an opportunity I couldn't pass up.

I sucked in a breath, hoping I'd convinced myself that Weston was no longer a threat to my heart. "Well, thank you again for everything you did tonight. I truly appreciate it."

He flashed a smile. "Anytime. I'll be seeing you around."

With a nod toward him, I stuck my key in the door and twisted the lock. When my apartment came into view, I let out a gasp.

Weston rushed back to me. "What is it?"

I pointed inside.

Even though I'd just unpacked yesterday, the contents of my apartment were strewn everywhere.

Somebody had wanted to send me a message.

They'd done so loud and clear.

I knew without a doubt that I wasn't welcome here.

DETECTIVE GARRISON ARRIVED at my house thirty minutes later.

Of *course*, it was Detective Garrison. He didn't look thrilled to be here any more than I felt excited to have him. He'd brought two other officers with him, and they were now searching my place for clues.

Garrison frowned as he stared through the doorway into my apartment. I hadn't touched anything—I knew better than to do that.

We'd been sequestered to the hallway so nothing would be tainted inside. Right now, the space felt stuffy and too small.

"Initially, I thought your purse snatching last night was just an isolated incident." Garrison rubbed his chin as he continued to stare inside my place. "Now, I'm not so sure."

"These events don't seem so random now, do they?" I tried to keep the smugness from my voice, but I wasn't sure I was successful.

"Not when you combine the purse snatching with this." Garrison shrugged, something close to resignation in his gaze. He'd wanted to be right, but now he was having trouble justifying his earlier actions.

"I also got a threatening note this morning," I told him. I'd thought about calling him earlier to tell him, but I hadn't. Now seemed like a good time.

"You got a note this morning?" Weston turned to me, a wrinkle on his brow.

Because, of course, he'd hung around as I'd waited for Garrison to arrive. Really, it was sweet, albeit unnecessary.

"I did." I turned back to Garrison. "It said that I wasn't welcome here."

Garrison stared at me. "Where exactly did you find this note?"

"Someone left it on my desk at the conservatory."

"Did you keep it?" The way he asked the question was slightly mocking, and I didn't appreciate it.

"As a matter of fact, I put it in my desk drawer. Just in case."

He narrowed his eyes, his resignation turning to irritation. "I'm going to need to see it, to see if any prints were left on it. Did you think about checking the security footage near your office to see who left it there?"

I crossed my arms over my chest and shrugged, knowing he had me on that point. "I thought about it, but I didn't actually do it yet. I had other things that took priority."

Garrison's eyes narrowed even more. "I'll do it for you. How about that?"

The man was getting territorial, wasn't he? I suppose I couldn't blame him.

Still, he was all over the place. Remorseful one minute. Irritated the next. What was up with this guy?

"Of course," I finally said. "Whatever you want."

He continued to stare at me. "Any reason you didn't report it?"

I shrugged, really wishing I could simply go into my apartment and unwind. That wouldn't be happening any time soon. Even when the place was released, I was going to have a lot of cleanup to do.

"I've received a lot of threats in my day," I told Garrison. "I figured one letter wasn't going to mean that much in the grand scheme of things."

Garrison let out a sigh and stared down the hallway as if taking a moment to compose himself. "If you get any more, please let us know. Do you have any idea why somebody might have sent you the note?"

"I don't."

Weston crossed his arms and leaned against the wall, listening to every single detail of our conversation but reserving his final thoughts until now. "Maybe it's because you're looking into Heather's death."

I sent Weston a death glare. That fact wasn't exactly something I wanted mentioned in front of the detective. Weston had known that, but he wanted to stoke the fire, didn't he?

Now, both of their gazes burned into me as they waited for my explanation.

I frowned. "I *have* been looking into Heather's death. But I have a hard time believing I've made anyone mad."

"As I've told you before, Heather's death was ruled an accident." Garrison's voice held barely contained exasperation.

I couldn't be positive, but I almost thought he viewed me as a threat. Why would that be?

"I think you guys are wrong." I paused and cast the detective a remorseful look. "No offense."

He ignored my last statement. "I'm not sure why you think Heather's death might have been a homicide."

"That stolen video just doesn't fit. It clearly shows there's more to the story."

"But why would anyone want to murder Heather?" Garrison continued watching me.

"That's what I'm trying to figure out."

"I have to discourage you from doing that," Garrison said. "If you're right, you might be putting yourself in danger."

"I'm aware of that, and I'm not here to investigate. I'm just asking questions."

Garrison gave me another pointed look. "Asking questions is always where it all starts."

I couldn't deny that. "Noted."

His words stayed in my head for the rest of the night.

Because "where it all starts" was another way of saying "where being nosy could get a person hurt."

CHAPTER SEVENTEEN

WESTON STUCK AROUND after Garrison left. Normally, I might grumble beneath my breath about him being here. But this time he was helping me straighten up, so I welcomed his company. "Many hands make light work" was one of my favorite sayings.

He paused by a bookshelf and picked up a picture of me and Phil at the Grammy Awards. Of all the photos I could have brought, I'd chosen that one.

I wasn't even sure why. Maybe I just wanted to be reminded of my past. Of where I'd been and where I was now. That was the last big event I did before leaving that part of my life behind.

"I still can't believe you walked away from this." Weston set the picture back on the shelf.

"I still can't believe I ever walked into it."

He let out a chuckle. "Touché."

I crossed my arms and leaned back against my couch. "It's just the truth."

Weston continued to study me. "Do you ever miss it?"

I didn't even have to think about my answer. "Nope. Not at all."

"Well, I guess it's the rest of us who are missing out. Nothing I love more than hearing you sing."

"I still sing. Just not onstage."

Weston paused and looked at me for a moment. I tried to read the look in his eyes before deciding I didn't want to know exactly what he was thinking.

If I searched deep inside myself enough, I'd probably admit I still needed to deal with the hard feelings I felt after things ended between the two of us. I didn't want those feelings to be there. I didn't want to be petty.

But I was skating around the bigger issues that stood between us.

Mostly, the heartbreak.

I'd been swept away by this man. Even Phil hadn't consumed me and infatuated me like Weston had. What we'd had between us seemed like that once-in-a-lifetime thing.

Weston straightened, looking as if he were about to say something important. "Camryn—"

Before he could finish, his phone rang. He let out a sigh then pulled the device from his pocket and glanced at the screen. "I've got to take this."

A surprising disappointment pressed on me. "Of course. Do what you need to do."

He put it to his ear and paced into the kitchen. But I could still hear his half of the conversation.

He was talking to Athena—his ex-wife.

"I understand what you're saying, but you can't do that," Weston murmured. "I've already planned to see them this weekend. I've already arranged everything."

When I heard the anguish in his voice, I began straightening a bookshelf and tried not to listen.

That wasn't entirely true. I *was* curious as to what he was talking about. Curious about what his relationship was like with his ex-wife.

His ex-wife who'd cheated on him with a tech mogul. The two of them were now married, and Weston had been publicly dumped and humiliated.

"I'm telling you, you can't do that. It's not fair." He paused near the window and stared out. As he did, his shoulders tightened, and he shook his head. "Then I'm going to call my lawyer. I don't want to get him involved again, but I will." Weston's voice rose with every new word.

He muttered a few more things. Seconds later, the call ended and Weston shook his head. His cheeks flamed red, and I knew his emotions were getting the best of him. I gave him a few seconds to compose himself.

Then I paused from straightening and turned to him. "Is everything okay?"

"That woman is impossible." He ran a hand through his hair, leaving the strands sticking out in various directions.

"You obviously loved her at one time," I reminded him. Maybe it wasn't the most sensitive thing to say, but considering he'd left me for her, how could I help myself?

"I guess I deserve that." He let out a puff of air as if he was annoyed with himself. "But I'm working hard to be a better man—and not just because that's the name of one of my songs."

I almost had to smile at that, but I didn't. "What's going on?"

He practically dropped into a chair at my kitchen table. "My time on the road took a toll on my family. I never cheated on Athena, but I know all the blame for our failed marriage isn't squarely because

Athena didn't remain faithful. She's determined to make me pay by keeping the kids from me. I'm only able to see them twice a month. I needed a more stable schedule, which is one of the reasons I got a job here."

"You moved here to be close to your kids . . . ?" Things began to click in my mind.

"That's right. They're great." His eyes grew warm. "Allison is eleven, and she's so full of life. And Tyler is thirteen, and he's beginning to act like a teenager."

"I remember those years well."

A sad smile tugged at his lips. "I'm sure you do. Parenting is hard. I don't want to feel like I've screwed up my kids' lives. Sometimes I think it might be too late."

"Keep trying. Keep letting them know you care. One day, they'll remember it." I had to admit I respected Weston for giving so much up for them.

Not that it *really* surprised me. Weston's character had impressed me at one time in my life, and I knew he wasn't a bad person. But he'd been sucked into the machine—one that was nearly impossible to get out of once you were in.

I knew firsthand the pitfalls of the music industry.

He rose and nodded toward the door. "Well, I

should get going and call my lawyer. The two of us need to have a long talk."

"Thank you for everything tonight. I really appreciate it."

"It's no problem." He paused in the doorway and stuffed his hands into the pockets of his jeans as he turned to me. "Be careful, and call me if you need me. You promise?"

I nodded. "I promise."

But I didn't plan on needing him.

I COULDN'T SLEEP after Weston left, so instead I pulled out my computer and did a quick search for any info on Langston Murphy.

His social media page appeared, and I scanned the information there. My eyes stopped on his latest update—which was just posted two days ago.

Langston and his band were performing at a local club in Savannah—tonight.

I glanced at my watch. It was almost eleven. The band was supposed to go on at nine.

Would they still be playing?

I didn't know. But this could be a good opportunity to talk to him, to find out why he'd run. If he was the one behind this, then he needed to stop before things escalated any further. The fact that my place had been ransacked showed this wasn't over yet.

Without wasting any more time, I secured an Uber and caught a ride to the club, which was located ten minutes from the campus.

As I stepped from the sedan, I heard rock music blaring from the brick-fronted building. People who looked to be college age lingered outside, and a bulky security guard stood near the door.

I tried not to cringe as I listened to the music. The band's rhythm was slightly off-tempo, and the singer screamed instead of singing. He was doing horrible things to his vocal cords right now, which would probably result in surgery later in his life.

Was this the kind of talent they were accepting at Grand Isle? If so, times truly had changed. And Langston was supposed to be an outstanding drummer. Outstanding drummers didn't play off-tempo like that.

I had a feeling I knew what I was going to find inside, but I had to see for myself anyway.

I pushed my way to the door and smiled at the guard there. "Need to see an ID?"

An amused sparkle filled his gaze, probably as he

soaked in the fine lines beginning to form at my forehead and the corners of my eyes. "I think you're okay."

At one time, the fact that I hadn't retained my youth would have disappointed me. But no more. I was going to embrace this new season and be thankful for the opportunity each new phase in life brought.

Some people never got these opportunities.

I slipped inside, *really* feeling out of place.

I definitely didn't fit in wearing my black skirt and ivory blouse.

Instead of focusing on the people around me, I headed toward the stage where a band played. They were too far away for me to make out many details.

But the overwhelming sounds inside the place made my heart pound harder.

Noise overload was a real concern with me, and, unless I kept myself focused, I might have something close to a panic attack.

After being jostled by several twenty-somethings, I finally reached the front and stared up at the performers onstage. My eyes scanned the singer, the bass player, the guitarist . . . and finally stopped on the drummer.

I frowned.

He wasn't Langston.

The name written across the bass drum read *Inner Fury*, and Langston played with *Rabid*.

It looked like this little excursion was all for nothing.

But, somehow, I had to figure out a way to track down this Langston guy.

Especially now that my life appeared to be on the line.

CHAPTER EIGHTEEN

EVEN THOUGH I hadn't learned anything about Langston last night, he remained at the top of my suspect list.

Still, I wanted to keep my options open. Maybe I was too obsessed with this. But considering the fact that my purse was stolen, a threatening note had been left, and my apartment ransacked, I felt like I had good reason.

As soon as I got to work the next morning, I called Skittles into my office and asked her to help me track down the name of the girl who'd eaten peanuts before singing into the mic that Heather Klein had used next.

The information wasn't public, but Skittles knew. Most of the student body did, apparently.

As soon as I heard the student's name, all the noises flatlined around me.

Jana Littleton.

She was one of the people Weston had mentioned as a front-runner in the talent competition.

That *definitely* made her a person of interest.

To my surprise, I discovered she was still on campus. I'd figured she might need some time at home after what she'd been through, but apparently not.

Was Jana hoping the talent show would still go on?

Was that because she'd risked everything to ensure she might win?

I didn't want to jump to any conclusions. Joel would tell me that was the top mistake investigators made. But the connection couldn't be denied.

I headed to her dorm. It was only ten a.m., and I knew Jana could still be sleeping. After all, she was a college student and she'd been through a lot.

I knocked and no one answered. But I heard someone inside. I heard the sheets rustling and a soft—maybe irritated—groan.

I knocked again, more urgently this time.

A moment later, the door flew open, and Jana

Littleton scowled at me. Her black hair fell into her eyes, the wedge cut probably ensuring her hair was always in her face. Her nails were painted black also, and tattoos decorated her arms.

Her expression softened slightly when she saw an adult standing there—but only slightly.

"Can I help you?" Her voice teetered on the edge of terse.

"I'm sorry to wake you. I know it's early. But I have a few questions that can't wait." I shifted. "I'm Camryn, by the way. I'm the new Chief Communications Officer here at Grand Isle."

Jana hesitated another moment, almost like she just wanted to close the door and pretend she hadn't heard me in the first place. But, finally, she opened it wider and allowed me to step inside.

Blackout shades had been pulled down over the windows, so it was still dark inside. If she had a roommate, I didn't see her. But I could smell a strange mix of incense and body odor in the room. I had a feeling Jana might be one of those all-natural type of people who didn't believe in deodorant.

Jana flipped on the light on a table before plopping on the couch and practically curling into a ball. I sat in the chair across from her—after I moved some dirty clothes from it.

This girl was clearly a slob.

"You live alone?" I started.

Jana rubbed her eyes, looking disinterested in my question. "No, I have a roommate, but she likes to stay at her boyfriend's place."

I licked my lips before starting, knowing that small talk would do no good here. "Jana, I need to ask you some questions about the talent show."

Her expression instantly sobered, almost as if she'd physically withdrawn. "What do you want to know?"

"First, you got food poisoning a few days ago?"

She nodded, her eyes nearly hollow. "I did. I ate some fish from a food truck. I should have known better."

"Did you go to the doctor?"

"No, thankfully, I only took a few bites of my food so I wasn't really, really sick."

"That's good. I'm glad you're better." I shifted. "I also heard you ate peanuts right before you sang."

She lowered her eyelids and glanced at her lap, her shoulders hunching downward. "That's my go-to snack. I'm doing keto. Trying to stay skinny. People say you have to be if you want to make it in this industry."

I'd heard that one before. "How long before you went onstage did you eat them?"

She shrugged. "Maybe thirty minutes. I didn't want to scarf food down backstage, so I ate before I went to Hannon Auditorium. I didn't even think anything of it." Her voice cracked, and she rubbed her throat.

I saw her wrestling with her emotions. With guilt. As anyone would in her shoes.

"Then you sang your song, which probably took ten minutes between warm-up and mic checks, is that correct?" I asked gently, not trying to upset her any more than she already was.

"I guess so. Heather went right after me. There must have still been particles—" A sob cut off her words, and she pressed her hands into her eyes as if trying to control herself.

"Do you have the bag of nuts you were eating?"

She glanced up and narrowed her eyes with confusion. "I do. But what does that have to do with this?"

"I'd like to see the bag if that's okay."

"I guess so." She stood, looking annoyed again. She stomped to the kitchenette, opened a cabinet, pulled out a bag, and handed it to me.

I studied the label a minute and narrowed my eyes. "Jana, these aren't peanuts."

She stared at me in disbelief, like I was an idiot adult of some sort. "Of course, they are. What else would they be?"

"They're cashews."

She let out a puff of air and shrugged. "Same smell, right? A nut allergy is a nut allergy, right?"

I wasn't so sure about that. But it was something I needed to look into.

I knew the perfect person to call to find out some information.

I stood. "Thank you for all your help."

"That's all you need to know?" She stared at me, tears welling in her gaze as grief and guilt flooded her again.

I knew all about those waves of emotions.

"That's all." I offered a soft smile, trying to let her know that I understood. "I'm glad you're still here."

"I was thinking about going home this weekend, just to get away for a while. But I'm hearing the talent show might still go on. Part of me thinks I shouldn't even try to be a part of it. But I've worked for a month to get my song ready to sing and . . ."

"I understand. I'm sure whatever decision you make people will understand."

Armed with this new information, I left the dorm. I needed to get to my office.

If my theory was right and there was a difference between a peanut allergy and a cashew allergy, then I may have found the smoking gun I needed to prove Heather's death was no tragic accident.

Also, Jana seemed remorseful. I didn't think she was the type to hurt someone on purpose.

Did that still leave me with Langston Murphy as my primary suspect?

It looked like it. I just needed to find him.

I CALLED MY SISTER-IN-LAW, Phil's sister, who just happened to be a doctor, and I posed my question about nut allergies. She confirmed my theory that not everyone allergic to peanuts was also allergic to cashews.

I didn't know where Heather fell within that spectrum, but I felt confident that there was more to the story. I even called Garrison and Joseph to let them know about my discovery. Garrison said he'd look into it further, and Joseph sounded almost disgruntled. Clearly, he wanted this to be an accident and not a homicide. I couldn't blame him.

From the dorm, I walked across campus toward the administration building. The campus was unusually quiet, but that wasn't surprising since classes hadn't started back up again. They wouldn't until Monday.

Just as I stepped inside the admin building, I nearly collided with someone.

"I'm so sorry—" My apology turned into a scowl when I looked up and saw who it was.

Oden McIntyre.

I'd like to say he looked surprised to see me, but he didn't. Had he been hoping to run into me?

"I heard you'd started here." He scanned me from top to bottom and then back again as if trying to measure how I'd held up through the years. I'm sure, in his opinion, I hadn't aged well.

I raised my chin. This man would not make me feel less than—even if the feat was a special talent of his. "I just came this week."

He clucked his tongue in disapproval. "What a waste of talent."

"Most people say that I'm pretty good at what I do." Fire subtly burned at the edge of my tone. This man wasn't going to trigger me, but it was going to take all my self-control to keep that from happening.

"I mean, your *musical* talent." He pursed his lips

and raised an eyebrow, not bothering to hide his annoyance.

"If there's something I've learned over the years it's that you've only got one life to live, so you've got to make choices you can live with. That's exactly what I did."

"My theory remains that this was all Phil's influence on you. If you'd never met him, you'd still be a star today." Disdain dripped from his words. "I should have never hired his company to protect you."

"If I was a star today, you'd be even richer than you already are." I knew what this really boiled down to. Oden was all about money. He couldn't get enough of it.

His eyes glimmered, showing he wasn't bothered at all by my proclamation. "A little cash never hurt anybody."

"Tell that to all the thieves who ended up in jail."

He chuckled as if my statement surprised him. "Aren't you funny? I've always known you were something special, Camryn Paine. And you still are. One day, I'll get you to realize that."

Something about his ominous tone made me shiver.

I thought of the anonymous note that had been

left on my desk. Someone thought I didn't belong here at Grand Isle. Someone wanted me to leave.

Would Oden go as far as to threaten me like that? If so, what would his motive be?

I didn't know.

But I couldn't rule him out either because he was the most cold-hearted person I knew.

CHAPTER NINETEEN

ODEN'S GAZE felt hot as he stared at me, and I wanted to poke him in the eyes. Not very mature of me, but even forty-somethings had their moments.

He raised his chin as if realizing he'd outlived his welcome. Then he took a step back. "Anyway, it's good to see you, Camryn."

"Will you be sticking around Grand Isle for a while?" I hoped he said no.

"As you probably know, I came here to judge the talent show. I'm still waiting to hear the board's final decision. Until then, I'm enjoying some time on Tybee Island." He observed me a moment before tilting his head. "If you get bored while you're in town . . ."

A snippy reply played on the tip of my

tongue. Something about how I would rather ride an elephant through the jungle in a rainstorm—don't ask me where I got that illustration. Before the words left my lips, someone spoke behind me.

"Oden," a man said. "I think someone's looking for you over in the Hannon Auditorium."

He gave me another suggestive glance before pulling his aviator sunglasses down over his eyes. "Good. Maybe I'll know whether or not I'm wasting my time here." He stepped toward the door. "I hope you have a great day."

I watched him walk away, trying to control the irritation simmering inside me. I wanted so badly for that man to be put in his place. But he seemed like the type who could do whatever he wanted and get away with it.

As Oden faded from sight, I turned to the man who'd essentially saved me from any more of Oden's jabs. I'd seen this guy at the staff and faculty meeting Joseph had called when I'd first arrived, but I hadn't been introduced to him yet.

He reminded me a bit of Tom Everett Scott, the actor. He was tall and thin with curly dark hair that had just a touch of gray. He had to be close to my age.

But his eyes were what caught my attention. They were brown, warm, and kind.

I offered a quick, grateful smile. "Thank you for that."

He shrugged as if it were no big deal. "Oden is a first-class jerk. He thinks he's better than everyone else, and that just irritates me."

"Was someone really looking for him in the Hannon Auditorium?"

"No, but I figured that would get rid of him for a while." A smile stretched across his face as he extended his hand. "My name is Mark White. I'm the Dean of Students here. I haven't had the chance to introduce myself yet."

"It's a pleasure to meet you," I told him. "I'm—"

"Camryn Paine." He shrugged, almost looking embarrassed. "You're the talk of the campus. That being said, you'd even be the talk of the campus if we hadn't had such a tragic turn of events this week."

My smile faded at the reminder of what had happened to Heather. "I know. I'm sorry about everything that's happened."

"We all are." He nodded down the hallway stretching in front of us. "I'm headed to the office. How about you?"

"Me as well."

"If you don't mind, I'll walk with you." He fell into step beside me.

I wouldn't complain. "Sounds great."

I let a moment of silence fall—silence other than our footsteps, a few people murmuring in the distance, and wheels across the tile floor—most likely, from a janitor.

"So, what do you think about everything that happened?" I couldn't seem to stop myself from asking that question. It seemed to come as naturally to me as, "How are you?"

"You mean about Heather's death?" Mark's pitch rose with surprise before dipping with sorrow. "It was tragic."

"You really think it was an accident?"

Maybe I was jumping into this too soon. I should have had more casual conversation first. But as I'd gotten older, I'd simply become more blunt. I didn't like wasting time with meaningless conversation—not when other things were on my mind, at least.

"That's what the police seem to have ruled. That's good news, right? That being said, it's not that we'd want anyone to die. But I'd hate if someone did this on purpose." Mark sounded truly astonished at the idea of there being a murder on campus.

I didn't say anything in response to that question. "Did you know Heather?"

"I had met her on several occasions. She seemed like a nice girl."

"Anything extraordinary about her?"

He slowed his steps as if he were thinking. "Let's see. She was a great singer—and she could juggle."

"How do you know that?"

He paused and casually rested his hands on his hips. "We have a new tradition at the school, one that started five years ago. It's kind of like the Gong Show where students must display a talent other than music. It's very entertaining."

"It sounds like it." I had to wonder what I might have contributed if we'd had that back when I'd been a student. I had learned to ride a unicycle not long ago . . .

"You should see Jinky. She can make her eyebrows dance."

"That's a thing?" I tried to picture it.

Mark smiled. "It is."

"I know I'll be Googling tonight."

"That being said . . ." Mark shifted, and his voice rose in pitch. "I *did* hear a rumor Heather had started a secret club."

His words caused my breath to catch, and I

paused. "A secret club?"

Mark shrugged, his eyes glimmering with curiosity. "Supposedly, it's all underground and top secret —which makes it even cooler. At least, it does to the students who participate."

I still wasn't following. "When you say club, do you mean something like a sorority or fraternity?"

"I mean, more like *Dead Poets Society* stuff. You know, to make it even more fun, they like to have secret passwords and handshakes and places to meet. Not for any good reason other than the fact that they think those things make their clubs more exciting."

"And you think Heather was involved in one of them?" Maybe this was another lead, another possibility as to what could have happened to her.

Mark called hello to a professor before turning back to me. "She came to me asking questions about my thoughts on it. These clubs aren't smiled upon by leadership here."

My mind continued to race. "Do you have any idea who else may have been a part of it?"

He started to answer, but before he could, a scream cut through the air.

The two of us glanced at each other before taking off down the hallway toward the sound.

CHAPTER TWENTY

I SPRINTED to the entrance of the girl's bathroom and flung the door open.

A student stood in front of me, her hand over her heart as she stared at something on the floor. I rushed past her to get a better look, Mark on my heels.

I sucked in a breath when I saw a brunette sprawled on the marble tiles.

I knelt on one side of the girl, Mark on the other. Wasting no time, I pressed a finger to her neck, trying to find a pulse.

I didn't feel anything.

"Call 911," I rushed.

We needed paramedics. Maybe they could revive her. Maybe it wasn't too late.

As Mark put his phone to his ear, I began doing CPR, trying to see if I could bring this girl back to life. The student who'd screamed remained in the doorway in shock, staring at us as if she didn't know what to do.

After several moments of chest compressions, Mark placed his hand over mine. I knew what he was doing.

He was silently telling me that it was too late.

He didn't have to tell me. I knew. I was just in denial.

I didn't want this woman to be dead.

Taking one last look at the girl—her slim figure, her brown hair, her pale skin—I stood. The weight of defeat pressed on my shoulders.

Instead of wallowing in the feeling, I turned to the girl by the door. "What happened? Did you see anything?"

She shook her head, tears welling in her eyes. "I don't know. I just walked in here, and I found Natalie like this."

I studied Natalie again, but I didn't see any signs of foul play on her body. There were no open wounds. No bruises. Nothing.

What happened to make another seemingly healthy college student just drop dead?

A bad feeling brewed in my gut.

Then I took a better look at the girl's face.

She was one of the students I'd seen leaving the candlelight vigil yesterday—one of the three who'd huddled together acting suspiciously.

My heart thumped into my ears.

I glanced at Mark, searching his face for any signs of recognition. "Do you know her?"

He frowned. "Natalie Manning. She's a freshman."

A freshman? That would make her the same age as my Scarlett. My heart pounded harder.

"Did she have any medical conditions?" I asked.

"None that I know of." Mark glanced at the door. "Look, we should get out of here to preserve the scene, just in case. We can stand outside to make sure no one gets in until the police and paramedics arrive."

I nodded. I'd been about to say the same thing. But I was trying to soak in as many details as I could first.

Mark ushered us out into the hallway.

By the time we got there, a crowd had already gathered, and they stared at the door as if the Chamber of Secrets waited on the other side.

Joseph Hannon split through the mob as he

rushed toward us. "What's going on? I heard some-thing happened."

Mark and I glanced at each other, and I knew I needed to take this question.

Because I was the one who was eventually going to have to deal with all this.

DETECTIVE GARRISON GLANCED at me as we stood in the entrance to the bathroom. "You found her?"

"Mark and I heard a student scream and came to see what was wrong," I started. "Speaking of which, the girl who found Natalie is waiting in my office. I figured you'd need to talk to her."

"I do." He shifted as he turned to face me. "By the way, I know my timing is off, but I was going to call you to let you know we recovered your purse. Someone found it in an alley about a half mile away from your apartment."

My heart lifted. "And they turned it in? You have it?"

He nodded. "I don't know what was in it in the first place, but the only things I noticed missing were your cell phone and keys. Your money and credit cards all appeared to still be there. But you can look at it and let us know for sure."

"Thank you. I'll come down to the station later."

He nodded and turned back toward Natalie's body. The medical examiner bent over her silently.

After a few seconds, he rose. "If I had to guess, she died of an overdose."

An overdose? How had he drawn that conclusion? "What makes you think that?"

"Grayish-purple skin, vomit, and mostly . . . the empty pill bottle that we found that had rolled from her hand into the corner."

I frowned. "Do you have any idea how long she's been dead?"

"My guess is at least an hour."

"And no signs of foul play?" I asked.

"Not that I can tell. No unusual bruising or signs that someone forced something into her. But the medical examiner will have to do the autopsy to know for sure."

"Excuse me," a new voice said. Joseph. "Could I borrow Camryn for a minute?"

Garrison scowled, as if annoyed by the interruption. "Of course. I'll find you if I need to."

Joseph motioned for me to follow him.

I knew that Mark was talking to some of Natalie's

classmates, doing his job as the Dean of Students. No doubt he was trying to keep them calm in the middle of this turbulent situation.

It was a good thing the grief counselors were still on campus.

Hannon pulled me into his office before I could say a word.

"Donors are already threatening to pull their support." As sweat spread across his forehead, he reached into the mini fridge against his back wall and grabbed a bottle of Perrier. He took a long sip before turning back to me, nearly breathless. "We can't let that happen."

"What would you like me to do about it?"

"How do we get ahead of this?"

"We can't do anything until Natalie's family has been notified. But as soon as that happens, we should be upfront about things before conjecture sets in—just like with Heather."

He nodded a little too quickly. "Okay. We can do that. But two dead students in a week? Three in the past month? I can't believe it. This is a nightmare. The only comfort I can find in this whole situation is the fact that the deaths don't appear to be homicides."

"You think two deaths in one week is coincidental?" Was he even listening to himself?

He stared at me for a moment, and I could see him processing my statement and carefully choosing his next words.

"If they weren't accidental, then what were they?" he asked.

I could tell by his tone that he didn't want to hear the truth. So, instead, I shrugged and took a step back. "I'm going to get to work on a press release. I assume you're going to call Natalie's parents?"

His face instantly sobered. "I will. As soon as the police chief gives me the okay."

"Okay then. You know where to find me."

CHAPTER TWENTY-ONE

I WALKED into my office and spotted the girl who'd found Natalie sitting there. An hour had passed, and she was still here. Alone.

Poor thing.

Tears ran down her cheeks as she sat across from my desk.

I lowered myself into the chair beside her and placed a hand on her arm. I should have never left her alone this long. But my meeting with Joseph had taken longer than I'd thought and . . .

I licked my lips. "What's your name?"

She sniffled. "Blake."

"I'm Camryn, Blake. Can I get you something? Some water or something to eat?"

She shook her head, her red eyes bearing the scars of shock and grief. "I'll be fine."

"Did you know Natalie?"

"Not really well, but we were in a couple of classes together. She seemed nice."

"What was she like?"

"She played the electric guitar, and she was amazing. Totally amazing. I don't even know why she had to come to this conservatory. She could have easily gotten a job straight out of high school. That's how talented she was."

I frowned. That made her a front-runner, didn't it? "As far as you know, did Natalie have any enemies? I know you said you didn't really know her but..."

She stared at me and blinked. "You think she was killed?"

"I'm not saying that." I needed to quickly backtrack. "I'm just trying to get a feel for who she was and who I need to tell."

I was nearly certain that explanation wasn't going to go over because it didn't make sense.

But Blake nodded. "We're in a school where everybody is in competition for the top spots. To be in a top spot practically guarantees you your pick at whatever career you want."

I swallowed hard. I should have remembered that from my time here. Maybe I had pushed those memories aside. I didn't want to live in a world where people would do anything to get ahead. But I knew that was what surrounded me. I wasn't naive.

I suppose I just wanted to somehow get away from it. But that wasn't possible.

Detective Garrison knocked on the door and nudged it open.

"I'd like to talk to you if that's okay." He nodded to Blake.

Panic seemed to swell in her—I could hear it as her breathing became shallower, as her eyes widened.

"Can Camryn stay with me?" she asked, glancing at me and practically begging for my approval.

Garrison sucked in a quick breath. If my hearing wasn't as good as it was, I wouldn't have noticed. But her question had thrown him off, and he seemed to scramble to figure out an answer.

Finally, he said, "If that's what you both want, then that's fine."

I nodded to let Blake know I'd stay with her.

Then Garrison pulled my chair from behind the desk, placed it in front of us, and began asking questions.

THREE HOURS later some of the chaos had subsided.

Natalie's body had been taken away by the medical examiner. The scene had been cleared. Students had been warned not to tell anybody until Natalie's family could be notified.

A few years ago, an accidental death occurred on the college campus near where I lived. Students posted their condolences online before the family had even been notified.

It had been a horrible way for them to find out information like that.

I'd heard a couple of students saying the pressure must have gotten to Natalie. In schools like Grand Isle, students were pushed to be their best. Most were Type A, driven, motivated, and their own worst critic.

Having pressure get to a student wouldn't be unheard of.

I knew Dr. Hannon had called Natalie's parents, but Mr. and Mrs. Manning were still trying to get up with other family members. As soon as her parents gave the okay, I'd distribute a press release.

As I sat at my desk, Jinky stuck her head into the doorway.

My office was in a prime area for anyone who wanted to swing by to chat.

It wasn't necessarily a bad thing, but the logistics might hinder me from getting work done.

She crossed her arms and pushed her tortoise-shell glasses higher on her nose. "Can you believe it? I'm totally obsessed with staying on top of all the gossip here at the school. I'm stunned, though. Absolutely stunned."

I twirled the pen in my hand between my fingers, wanting something to keep them busy. "I think we all are."

"Natalie just started here and was so excited."

"Just started?"

"After Velvet died, another spot opened up here at the school. Natalie was first on the wait list. She said it was a dream come true. Now . . ." Jinky frowned. "This place used to feel so safe."

But did it? Grand Isle had a bit of a sordid history. A few of the buildings on campus weren't original to the conservatory. In fact, one of them had been a mental hospital back in the early 1900s.

I knew it sounded cliché, but it was true. The

beautiful antebellum architecture was a wonder. Instead of tearing it down, the place had been converted into a dorm. The rest of the campus was built around that building.

Still, back when Jinky and I were students, things *had* felt safer.

Other than when Jennifer had disappeared.

I bit back a frown.

"Don't you ever just want to turn back time and go back to the way things used to be?" Jinky got a far-off look in her eyes as she stared at the wall in the distance. "I'm kind of obsessed with the idea of time travel. In fact, I heard there's a scientist who's on the verge of a breakthrough that will let us do that one day . . ."

Was she talking about time travel like it might really happen? "Did you hear that on the internet?"

She pushed her glasses up higher on her nose and straightened, almost as if my statement had surprised her. "I did. But wouldn't it be great? I felt so carefree back then."

I thought about Jinky's statement a moment before shrugging. "I don't know if I would do that or not. Don't get me wrong, I would love to see Phil again. To have him back. But . . . youth is filled with a lot of curiosity, ignorance, and heartbreak."

Her expression sobered. "Yes, I suppose it is. I guess I just choose to remember the good times."

"Or maybe that's the way that it should be."

"Or . . . what do they say? Those who forget history are doomed to repeat it? Does that mean I'm going to be left at the altar again?" Jinky let out a nervous laugh.

I glanced at my notes and held them up. "I don't want to cut this short, Jinky, but I have a press release to write."

She straightened from leaning against the doorframe. "I understand. Just one more thing. Have you run into Oden yet? I heard he's still hanging around."

My gaze darkened. "As a matter of fact, our paths crossed earlier. I don't think he's changed one bit. Whose idea was it to bring him in for this?"

"Joseph's. I mean the students are always beyond excited whenever Oden's name is mentioned. He *is* a star-maker." She said the words in a singsong manner to imitate the pedestal the students had put him on.

"When you're their age, it's easy to want to do whatever's necessary to make sure your dreams come true."

As my words hung in the air, I couldn't stop thinking about them.

Had someone been set on whatever was necessary to win this talent competition?

CHAPTER TWENTY-TWO

TWO HOURS LATER, after successfully sending out my press release, I sat in my office, my thoughts still turning over.

My mind wouldn't leave Heather's and Natalie's deaths.

Rebecca and Ned needed resolution, as did Natalie's parents. The killer needed to be caught. And if I ever wanted to feel safe again, I needed to figure out who was behind these crimes and had sent those threats.

I dipped one of my carrots into some mustard and listened to it crunch in my mouth as I chewed on my thoughts.

There was one angle I hadn't fully covered yet— one that I needed to examine further.

The talent show front-runners.

I'd gone through the list with Weston, but I needed to reexamine it.

First, there was Jordan Sawyer. He was a rapper who'd tripped going down the stairs and broken his leg. His injury hadn't totally taken him out of the talent show, but he'd headed home to recover. He'd been gone for the past week.

Then there was Jana Littleton. She had a case of food poisoning but had recovered in time to practice for the show. Though it had initially looked like she might have purposefully left peanut dust on the microphone cover, that wasn't the case. She'd been eating cashews, and she seemed truly remorseful about what had happened.

The final person was Beck Tarsus, a singer/songwriter and guitar player. He'd been in a car accident last week but had walked away.

Quickly, I did an internet search on him. The student had a great stage presence, a killer voice, and was handsome to boot. In fact, in some ways, he reminded me of Weston.

It turned out his band was playing at the Trills and Thrills Ball tomorrow.

That might be the perfect time to check him out.

There was also Langston. I wasn't ready to rule

him out yet. I just needed to find him and ask him a few questions.

There was also the death of Velvet Matthews. She'd supposedly died after slipping and hitting her head on the bathtub. But what if there was more to that story?

I'd continue to look for answers because I didn't believe these events were all accidents—no matter what Garrison said.

I was managing this crisis … my own way.

Unless these incidents stopped, the school would be in serious trouble.

WHEN I LEFT the campus that evening, I was alone.

It was dark outside, and I was exhausted.

Any other time, Weston would have appeared out of thin air and insisted on walking me home.

But he'd been surprisingly absent from campus today. Was that because he was dealing with his ex-wife? Had he contacted his lawyer about the joint custody issue and called some type of emergency meeting?

I didn't know.

Last night, as I'd listened to Weston speaking

about his children, I'd known without a doubt he loved them and that he'd do anything for them.

Most of us had people in our lives we'd do anything for. Our kids. Our spouses. Maybe our careers or reputation.

And maybe for some students, their futures.

I couldn't get that theory out of my head, and I wondered if I might be onto something.

I also wondered if this secret group Heather met with was somehow part of this whole mess. If Heather was involved in the group as well as our newest girl, then all kinds of suspicions flared to life in my mind.

There were so many possibilities. I really needed to narrow them down.

As I headed along the sidewalk, I glanced at the beautiful campus around me. This place still held secrets, even after all these years. I used to stand in Grand Isle's historic cathedral and press my hands into the stone walls. I would ask them to speak to me. Of course, I didn't think they would. I didn't think there were hidden messages just waiting to whisper secrets to me in the quiet moments. I wasn't superstitious like that.

But, still, I knew the buildings had stories to tell—stories I wanted to hear.

As my shoes clicked on the sidewalk, my phone chirped. An unknown number flashed on my screen, but that wasn't unusual since I'd lost my original phone. My temporary cell phone number had already been added to the online staff directory.

I hit Talk and put the device to my ear. But before I could even say hello, a digital voice crackled through the line.

"Mind your own business. I don't want to escalate this. But I will."

Instantly, I tried to memorize the sound. I never forgot a voice. But the caller was clearly trying to disguise his or her tone and had used a voice enhancer to distort it.

My blood went cold. "Who is this?"

But it was too late. The line was dead.

As I put the phone back in my purse, I glanced around, suddenly feeling like I was being watched.

I didn't see anyone's eyes on me, nor did I hear any approaching footsteps. Only buildings, a horse and carriage in the distance, and a group of college students talking too loudly on the other side of the street.

I had a feeling that the closer I came to answers the more danger I was going to be in.

CHAPTER TWENTY-THREE

FIFTEEN MINUTES LATER, I stepped into my apartment and paused. I placed my keys on a little table by the door and flicked a light on.

But nothing happened.

I knew enough to realize that was never a good sign.

Something inside me told me I should step back and run. Call the police. Call Weston. Call *someone* and have them check my place out.

But, instead, I listened.

I didn't dare breathe because I didn't want anything to hinder what I heard—not even my own inhaling and exhaling.

That's when I heard it.

The sound of someone else breathing. It was subtle. Soft.

But it was there. I was sure of it.

If I had to guess, the sound came from my living area. Maybe even from the other side of the wall, where I turned the corner to go into my kitchen.

My throat constricted and perspiration popped out over my forehead as I considered my options.

I was many things, but I wasn't a fighter. All the self-defense classes in the world wouldn't protect me now.

I had to get out of here.

Now.

I took a step back and grabbed the door handle.

But before I pulled it open, I heard footsteps closing in.

I was too late.

I should have left when the instinct had first hit me.

Someone wearing all black shoved me away from the door and against the wall.

I froze, waiting for some type of assault.

Instead, the figure threw the door open and darted from my apartment. I stared after him, still frozen with fear.

I willed my heart to slow down and my thoughts to focus.

What are you doing, Camryn? You can't let that person get away.

I rushed to look out my front door, but I realized the figure was gone. I was too late.

Or was I?

I grabbed the phone from my purse and quickly dialed 911.

The police station wasn't far away. Maybe the cops could find the person who'd been in my apartment.

Maybe they could also figure out exactly what this person had been doing.

Because if he wasn't here to hurt me, then he was here to do something else. I needed to figure out what.

"YOU DIDN'T GET a good look at him?" Detective Garrison stared at me as he stood in the hall outside my apartment.

His guys were inside looking for any fingerprints or other evidence.

This seemed like a repeat of a couple of nights ago.

Unfortunately.

"He was wearing all black, and it happened fast," I told Garrison. "But I'd guess this guy was close to two hundred pounds, not very athletic, and maybe even has asthma."

Garrison stared at me, a dumbfounded expression on his face. "Come again?"

I let out a breath before explaining. "I listen to people walk all the time, and I'm pretty good at guessing weight. I said not very athletic because this person wasn't light or graceful on his feet. And asthma? That's because I heard a slight wheeze."

"So, you gathered all that information just from listening?"

I nodded. "It's what I do."

He stared at me another moment before squinting. "If you're right, you have a very special talent."

I wasn't sure about that. Instead of agreeing, I shrugged. "Depends on how you look at it."

"Any idea why someone would break in . . . again?" Garrison continued.

"I suppose I *may* have been looking into Heather's death still," I admitted. Then I waited for his reprimand—not that it would do any good.

"That's not a smart idea."

"There's more to what's happening on campus. I know it, and I can't let it go. I can't believe that you would." Subtle irritation licked at the edges of my voice. I glanced around, saw no one, but I lowered my voice anyway. "Why *aren't* you looking into this more? I don't get it. You've got to know there's more behind these deaths."

His gaze flickered to his officers inside my apartment before he turned back to me. "I don't like what's happening any more than you, okay?"

That might be true, but . . . "That still doesn't explain why you're sitting back while students are dying."

"I'm not sitting back." His voice came out with a hiss. He seemed to realize how he'd sounded and let out a sigh. "I'm doing my best. I'm the new guy on the team, and my colleagues don't allow a lot of grace for newbies. One wrong move could ruin my career just as it's starting."

"Not acting on this could be your worst move."

He pressed his lips together, clearly contemplating what to say next. "Look, my father is friends with Joseph Hannon."

"Okay . . ." I wasn't sure where he was going with this.

Irritation flickered in his gaze. "Hannon is putting a lot of pressure on us to find the deaths as accidental."

"What?" My voice pitched higher as I tried to make sense of what he said.

"It's true. Hannon doesn't want the bad press for the conservatory."

"I know he brought me in for PR, but this is taking things too far!" I realized I was raising my voice and paused, sucking in a deep breath.

Garrison stepped closer. "I guess he wants to cover all his bases."

I wanted to argue, but I couldn't. Because I could totally see Joseph doing this. Using his power and influence to get his way.

But I didn't like it.

I remembered the figure in my apartment.

Two hundred pounds. Nonathletic. Asthmatic.

Those all fit Joseph.

Could he be behind this? Or was he trying to silence me so I wouldn't keep pushing to find answers?

It was a theory worth investigating.

"HAVE YOU SEEN THAT BOY ANYMORE?" I leaned back into the couch and held my breath as I waited for Scarlett's answer.

Detective Garrison had left, my apartment had been cleared, and I desperately needed to know that my daughter was okay. That's why I'd called her.

Ever since I'd seen Natalie, I'd been thinking about Scarlett. Thinking about how I would feel if I got the same call Natalie's parents had. I didn't even want to imagine it.

"No, I haven't seen my supposed stalker," Scarlett said. "Maybe I was just being paranoid."

I hated when other people dismissed their instincts as paranoia—even though I did it myself on occasion. "But maybe you weren't. You still need to be on the lookout."

"I will, *Mom*."

Scarlett said the words like only a daughter could to her mom. If a person could hear an eye roll, then that's precisely what I had just heard.

"Now enough about me." Scarlett switched the subject. "How are things with your new job? You keep wanting to talk about me, but I want to know about you."

Various thoughts raced through my mind, but I didn't want to burden my daughter with any of them.

It wasn't her job to worry about me. At least, not in this phase of life. She had enough on her mind without feeling the need to take care of her mom.

"It's a bit strange to step back into a place that played such a big role in my formative years." I took a sip of my water and kicked my shoes off, wishing I had someone nearby capable of giving a nice neck rub and foot massage. "But I think it's going to be good for me."

"I'm glad to hear that. I miss you. I can't wait to see you at Thanksgiving."

"It's just five weeks away. I can't wait to see you either." This was the longest I'd ever been away from her.

"Are we still going to go to Uncle Joel's?"

We'd made tentative plans with my brother this year. "That's the plan. But I haven't heard from him since he left for Costa Rica. I'm hoping he'll be back in time."

"It must be some job he's doing down there."

He'd been hired to protect the daughter of a CEO who'd been threatened. Joel did the type of work both Phil and his business partner, Zeke, had done when they'd started the company. "Yes, it really must be. You take care of yourself and call me if you need me."

"I will, Mom. I love you."

"I love you too."

After I ended the call, I held the phone to my chest. Funny how much things could change. How you could go from having a full life with family to being alone.

For a while, I let that fact bother me. Then I realized I needed to take action, that I'd only be as lonely as I allowed myself.

It was one of the reasons I'd taken the job here at Grand Isle. Life was too short to feel sorry for myself. I was only forty-three. My life was far from over.

In fact, in some ways I was in a much better place now than I had been before. Not that I would ever wish for Phil to have passed.

However, there was something empowering about being in your forties. About knowing who you were. About knowing your strengths and weaknesses.

I liked the fact that I no longer cared what people thought of me. I liked the fact that I didn't have to chase trends. And I especially liked the fact that I didn't have to worry about men.

Again, that didn't mean anything against Phil. I'd loved him deeply.

But finding the strength inside me to face the future by myself made me feel a rush of adrenaline.

This was my time. I didn't have to rush home to fix dinner for anybody. Didn't have to worry about anyone's laundry but my own or about keeping a clean house in case company stopped by. I didn't have to plan vacations with everybody else in mind or work my weekend plans around Scarlett's extracurricular schedule.

Those things had comprised a very sweet, precious time in my life.

But, right now, I had no choice except to move on, so I might as well embrace it.

That was one more reason I wanted to give this investigation my all.

CHAPTER TWENTY-FOUR

I HAD several things to take care of in the office the next morning. Things concerning my actual job description. I'd already met with Joseph, who was still a sweaty, nervous wreck.

The news had run a story on the three deaths here at Grand Isle, asking what was behind these "accidents." Accidents was in quotations because that was the tone of the entire piece. Some students from the school had even been interviewed and mentioned how spooked they felt.

The story had ended with: Were these deaths truly accidents or is something more sinister going on at the school?

I frowned as I watched the story for the fifth time.

Had the reporter, a thirty-something man named Abe Nowlin, called me to verify any of the information?

No.

That meant I was going to need to call Abe and ask for a retraction since the story contained conjecture.

Phones at the school were ringing off the hook. Several parents said they were coming this weekend to take their kids home until this was all resolved. Joseph was sweating bullets.

I couldn't stop thinking about everything that had happened.

And I couldn't stop thinking about what Garrison had told me about Joseph pressuring police to rule these deaths as accidental.

My old friend didn't have anything to do with this, did he?

I prayed the answer was no. I also prayed I'd make the right choice about whether I should ask him about it.

We had a board meeting later today that I'd been requested to attend. I wanted to see how Joseph handled things there. Sometimes, you had to know when to show your cards, and other times you had to know when to keep them hidden. That's what Phil had always said.

Right now, I was keeping what I knew quiet.

Tonight, I wanted to find Beck Tarsus and talk to him. I didn't want to think that he was sabotaging the competition for this talent show, but that was my best guess at this point.

However, his size didn't match the size of the intruder at my house last night. He wasn't large enough, nor did he appear to have asthma. Was he working with someone else?

The fact that I couldn't find Langston was a huge red flag itself. But I was running out of options as to ways to track him down. I did, however, see his name pop up on the school's online portal. He'd reserved a practice room for later today, and I planned to be there when he showed up.

And what about that secret club that Mark White had mentioned Heather being a part of? I wasn't sure if it had any relevance to all this or not. But I also needed to keep that fact in the back of my mind.

As I turned the thoughts over in my head, Skittles wandered into my office and took a seat in front of me.

I glanced at my assistant and the yellow candy in her bowl. Today was yellow?

I leaned back in my seat and turned toward her. "So, you pick what color you eat based on your mood for the day."

Her eyebrows shot up, and her hand froze mid-reach over the wooden bowl of candy. She stared at me, a touch of awe in her gaze. "How'd you know that?"

I shrugged. "It took me a couple of days to figure it out. Yellow must mean you're happy."

She gawked, grabbed some candy, and popped another piece in her mouth. "I'm impressed."

"Purple I'm guessing is melancholy. You were eating that color the first day I met you, right after Heather died."

"Also right."

"Orange . . . orange is a little harder." I tapped my lip with my finger as I stared at her. "But I'm thinking maybe it has to do with creativity. You were eating that color when you were planning the Trills and Thrills."

Her eyes lit. "You're really good. What do you think green is?"

"The obvious is envy."

"Right again. And red?"

"Love?"

She shook her head. "Nope, not love."

"Anger?"

"Nope."

I thought another moment before shrugging. "Then what?"

"Passion."

I nodded slowly. "How interesting. Why not a color for love?"

"Because love covers all those other emotions. Love brings happiness, creativity, sometimes melancholy, and definitely passion."

"Does love bring envy?"

"It shouldn't. But sometimes it does anyway."

I couldn't argue with her words. Love—especially imperfect love—could bring about some misplaced emotions at times.

Was love somehow the motivation behind these crimes?

Love of music? Romantic love?

I wasn't sure. But Skittles was right. Almost everything went back to love—however misplaced.

TWO HOURS LATER, I headed toward the practice rooms to see if Langston had shown up to use the space he'd reserved. But the area was like a ghost town.

"Everyone is headed to get ready for the Trills and Thrills Ball," a student called on her way out, almost as if reading my mind. "It's all hands on deck."

I thanked her for the update, but I didn't bother to leave the area. The soundproof rooms had a certain appeal to me. I used to come here to get away when I needed to find some calm in the midst of overwhelming sounds around me.

I paused by one and pushed the door open. The space was empty.

I'd spent many, many days in these rooms practicing. Wanting to be the best. Some type of unknown force had driven me to succeed.

On a whim, I slipped inside and shut the glass-fronted door. I stared at the piano against the wall, feeling as if my past was attempting to draw me back. After a moment of hesitation, I lowered myself on the bench in front of the piano.

It had been a long time since I'd played or sang. But being here at the school had brought back all kinds of memories for me. All kinds of old desires that I thought were totally dead.

I glanced through the glass door again and saw the hallway was still empty. I nibbled on my lip before tentatively placing my fingers over the keys. Then I played a C chord. I tried not to cringe when I noticed the key was out of tune. Probably nobody else would notice but me.

I closed my eyes as my hands began to take on a mind of their own.

Before I realized what was happening, I began playing *I've Never Loved Somebody Like You*. It was a ballad I'd written when I was only twenty-one. Back when I thought that love was the answer to everything. And maybe it was, in some ways.

But we couldn't look for others to solve our problems. If we weren't right with ourselves then nobody else would ever fill those gaps in us. I figured that was a lesson that some people couldn't learn until they had experienced it. Maybe I'd been one of those people.

As the song captured me, I sang the haunting lyrics I'd written so long ago.

You saw me in the shadows
Trying to blend in there.
It changed my world

Just to know you cared.
Then I stepped into the light
And into my own.
I gave you my heart
With abandon like I've never known.
I've never loved somebody like I love you.
I feel on top of the world.
I've come into the light,
Into the light,
Into love . . .
I've never loved somebody . . . like I love you.

I heard a step behind me and flinched, nearly jumping away from the piano as if it were on fire.

When I glanced back, I saw Weston peering into the room. He shrugged sheepishly. "I didn't mean to interrupt. I walked past and saw you inside. I knocked, but you were too caught up in the song to notice. It was just so good to hear you sing again."

I frowned and waved at the piano as if it had betrayed me. "I didn't think anybody was around so . . ."

"I wish you wouldn't stop playing on my account."

My cheeks flushed in a way I wished they wouldn't. "I should have never even done this. I mean, considering everything on my To Do List, I chose now to sit down and sing?"

He stepped fully into the room and crossed his arms. Not in an intimidating way, but in a way that made him look casual. "Maybe you just needed some type of stress relief."

I wanted to deny his words, but I couldn't. He was right. Music, when it wasn't the driving force in my life, was something that had made all my tension go away . . . for at least a few minutes.

Weston knew I'd written that song about him. We'd been dating at the time, but we broke up shortly after.

That's what made the song feel even more ironic.

"You and I spent a lot of time in here." His voice dipped to a lower, more intimate level.

That's probably because writing songs together felt like an intimate task. Music had drawn our souls together and threaded them into a symphony that very few could understand.

But that was the old part of my life, the part I wanted to put behind me. I wished Weston hadn't brought it up.

I'd felt a moment of connection with him, but I quickly shoved those thoughts aside. Especially when I remembered the woman I'd seen Weston with at the candlelight vigil. She was most likely his girlfriend. I had no right to feel anything right now.

Besides, I'd just claimed victory because I was no longer caught in the trap of being guy crazy or feeling like I needed a man's approval. Now, the next instant, I was feeling a rush of attraction.

I wiped my hands on my skirt as I stood. "I really should get back to work now."

Weston didn't say anything, but I felt his eyes on me. On my every move.

Before he could try to convince me otherwise, I slipped past him.

But I didn't feel like I could fully breathe until I was back in my office with the door closed.

AS I SAT in my chair nibbling on my carrots and mustard, my mind drifted back in time.

Back to when Weston and I had been together, and I'd been head over heels in love with him.

Our years together here at Grand Isle had been some of the best.

Then we'd both gotten recording contracts. The first few months had been fine. We'd been living off adrenaline, and any free moment we had we would fly back and forth to see each other.

Then we'd gone on tour—not together but separately. Trying to see each other during those times felt nearly impossible. Not only that, but the pressure of being in the limelight had gotten to me. I'd wanted to give up everything. But everybody told me I couldn't pass up the opportunity at fame.

Then the rumors started. Pictures of Weston with other women had appeared in various magazines. Not *with them*, with them. But photos of him having dinner. Of him having intimate conversations while sitting on park benches. Of him walking on the beach at sunset with a woman by his side.

The images could have been innocent, but as the frazzle of my nerves had mingled with the stress of my career, insecurity got the best of me. I'd felt pressures and demands coming at me from every angle.

So I'd told Weston that we should take a break until we could figure things out.

The thing was, Weston had said I was the only girl he'd ever love.

For that reason, I hadn't expected him to date someone else only two months into our break. When I'd said break, I'd really thought we'd temporarily spend some time apart. Maybe I'd taken a page out of Rachel and Ross's playbook from *Friends*. I wasn't sure. But I hadn't been talking about being apart forever—just until we could figure things out.

But apparently Weston hadn't seen things that way.

He'd met Athena Roland. Even though she was an in-demand model, her schedule was apparently much more flexible than mine. The next thing I knew, the two of them were dating and serious.

Not only that, but gossip magazines had started rumors that Oden and I were also together even though we weren't. Oden, who was twenty years my senior, never refuted those claims.

Weston and I had a few hard conversations before we called it quits. I'd cried my eyes out. Felt like my world had ended. I'd been certain I'd never find any joy in my life again.

Six months later, Oden hired a private security firm to do security for my concerts.

That's when I'd met Phil.

He wasn't one of my bodyguards, but he ran the company that managed my security team. He and his best friend—a former Marine—had started it. Zeke had been the tactical guy while Phil ran the business side of things. Phil had been steady. Level-headed. Pragmatic.

Everything Weston wasn't.

Phil and I had gotten married six months later.

A knock at my door jostled me from my thoughts.

I looked up and saw Skittles there.

It was probably better she'd interrupted my walk down memory lane. I had too much to juggle right now without revisiting that heartache of my past.

CHAPTER TWENTY-FIVE

SKITTLES STOPPED by my office before she left for the day. "Are you ready for Trills and Thrills tonight?"

I shrugged. I figured I'd at least make an appearance. It would be a good opportunity to get a feel for the student body, as well as listen to Beck Tarsus.

And maybe even to look for a killer.

"Ready for it? I'm not sure." I leaned back in my office chair. "Tell me about the event."

Skittles' eyes lit. "I'm on the committee for it this year, and it's going to be so much fun. I mean, part of me feels bad still having it after everything that's happened. But there's another part of me that's super excited because we put so much time and energy into it."

"Back when I went here, we all got dressed up and walked down a red carpet where everyone took pictures of us, and then we danced and ate fancy food."

"The red-carpet thing is so archaic." Skittles put a hand over her mouth as if embarrassed. "Sorry. I didn't mean to insult you."

I tilted my head and studied her, feeling lost . . . and old. "It's archaic?"

She shrugged. "I mean, things are just different now. We don't do the crazy red-carpet thing anymore."

"Do you still get dressed up?"

Her eyes twinkled. "We do. But it's different. We get dressed up and then accent our fancy outfits with something a little hillbilly since it's a harvest theme."

"Define hillbilly."

She shrugged. "You know, plaid or braided hair or straw in the mouth. Just something to make the event a little different from your average everyday ball. Oh, and the event is outside now."

"I'm going to assume there will be pumpkins and hay bales and apple cider?"

"Of course. We'll have some live music. There will be dancing. It's going to be a great time. You *are* going to be there, aren't you?"

I nodded. "Yes, although I need to figure out what to wear."

"I could help you ..."

I imagined how Skittles might dress me and politely declined, especially as I pictured myself dressed in a mix of K-Pop and hillbilly.

She started to stand but paused. "Three people have died on campus in the past month." Her voice was grim now, all signs of humor gone. "Do you think we should be worried? I mean, do you think something's going to happen tonight at the Trills and Thrills Ball?"

I nibbled on the inside of my lip as I tried to carefully choose my words. "There's a risk in everything, so I can't sit here and tell you that it's going to be perfectly safe. That said, it will probably be fine."

"Do you really think that these students have been dying of non-homicidal causes? That's what everybody on campus is talking about. Nobody can believe this."

"It is unnerving what's happened, but I know that the police are working on it."

"Everybody in the talent competition is really freaked out," she continued. "They're the ones who seem to have targets on their backs."

I straightened. "Did something else happen?"

"Not that I know of. I'd say enough has happened."

I nodded slowly. I couldn't argue with what she said. She was right.

Dead right.

THE MEETING with the entire executive board was that afternoon. I'd known it was coming, and I wasn't looking forward to it.

Joseph was there, of course, as well as everybody else in leadership at the school.

We needed to discuss everything that had happened and figure out how we would proceed.

Also, normally when one student dropped out, there was a waiting list of other students who would take their place. We officially now had three students who weren't a part of our curriculum any longer due to unforeseen circumstances, AKA death.

That meant we had two openings since Natalie had officially taken Velvet's place. And there hadn't been time to fill the other spot before Natalie's death.

It seemed a shame that people had to die for others to have these kinds of opportunities.

I listened during the meeting and took notes about what I needed to do to ensure the school maintained a positive reputation. I also interjected my professional opinion about being upfront and making sure students' safety and well-being was our priority.

"Are you still looking for answers?" one of the trustees asked me.

I hesitated before answering in front of such a large group. "I am. I've narrowed down my suspects, and I've been in communication with the police."

"Do you care to share these suspects with us?" Joseph asked.

Considering the fact his name was on the list, that didn't seem like such a good idea. "I prefer not to throw anyone under the bus."

"But you do believe these incidents haven't been accidents?" another trustee asked.

"I do."

"We don't want to jump ahead of ourselves." Joseph cast a pointed look at me.

He silently warned me not to say any more.

In the end, it was decided that the talent show would take place the next evening as scheduled. Several people had argued that the event was important to the school and to the students. Plus, Oden was already here and ready to be a guest judge. Since he was a maker or breaker of careers, most students felt like there was too much on the line to pass up this opportunity.

I had mixed feelings on the matter, but I was okay with whatever they decided.

Except I wasn't okay with Oden. But bringing him here hadn't been my choice, so I would need to live with it.

The meeting took up four hours of my day. Too many hours in my opinion. After we were done, I had the opportunity to do a few more things in my office before I needed to head home and get changed.

The Trills and Thrills Ball would start soon, and I needed to figure out something to wear. Then I needed to go so I could observe Beck Tarsus.

Whatever was happening here on campus needed to come to an end.

The best way to make that happen was to figure out who was behind it.

CHAPTER TWENTY-SIX

BACK AT MY APARTMENT, I pulled on a little black dress. If in doubt, a black dress was always a go-to.

I stared in the mirror. I was no longer a size four. To be honest, that had always been a struggle anyway. But I was a comfortable size ten. Even so, my body wasn't the same. It had filled out in some ways, and no amount of exercise and dieting would ever make me look the way I used to.

Truthfully, I'd hated trying to maintain that look.

With my job today, I still had to care about my appearance, so I tried to watch what I ate. I tried to walk every day. But I was no longer obsessed with food.

Besides, whoever had penned the term "perfect

size six" didn't know what they were talking about. There were plenty of perfect size eights, tens, twelves, fourteens, and up out there.

I stepped back, my thoughts racing back to the present.

I needed to add something to the outfit for the trills and thrills theme, but my mind went blank.

After looking through my closet, I found an old straw hat I wore at the beach and placed it on my head. It didn't scream hillbilly, but I didn't have much that would. I also grabbed an old black-and-white flannel shirt and tied the edges in a knot to make it more fitted.

This was going to have to work.

I slipped on some flats—heels killed my feet, and I didn't wear them unless I absolutely had to—and I started toward the party. Again, I was going to walk, but I didn't mind.

I especially didn't mind walking here in Savannah, my favorite city I'd ever lived in. There was so much art, culture, and history in this one town that it was hard to put into words just how fascinating the place was.

As I walked, I glanced around to look for any more signs of trouble. Clearly, someone thought I was suspicious of them. Otherwise, why would they be sending me these threats? My theory was the only thing that made sense, and that meant I needed to be on guard.

That's what Phil would want me to do.

Oh, Phil . . . I wasn't sure what he would think about everything that was happening here. Would he tell me to stay out of this? Probably. He'd always been protective of me.

One of the things I missed the most about him was being able to sit down together and run through our days. Being able to ask him for advice. He was the best advice giver I'd ever met.

The hard part about that was realizing that you'd never get those days back. He hadn't gone away for a long trip where we could reconnect afterward. Where we could resume life as normal after a given period.

It had been three years, and sometimes I still caught myself forgetting that. When I did, the grief came fresh all over again.

As I heard a truck pull up beside me, my muscles tensed. But when I glanced over, I saw Weston hanging his head out the window. "Need a ride?"

I waved him off. "I'm fine. I like getting in my steps."

"Are you sure? You probably have another two

miles until you get to the area where the Trills and Thrills is being held."

I glanced at the street ahead and frowned. As comfortable as these flats were, I wasn't looking forward to walking two miles in them. Finally, I shrugged and said, "Okay. If you insist."

He pulled to the side of the street, and I hopped in his truck. As soon as I did, Weston's scent filled my senses. It was the same as it had always been. A little bit of leather, a little bit of evergreen, and a whole lot of sexy.

"I'm surprised you're not driving there." Weston glanced at me, curiosity in his gaze. "You really like getting your steps in that much?"

I shrugged, not really wanting to get into the reasons why I didn't have a car or drive any longer. "This phase of life is perfect for walking, so that's what I'm doing."

He stared at me and nodded before shrugging. "Whatever floats your boat."

I glanced at his cowboy hat and cowboy boots and plaid shirt. "You really didn't have to do much to get dressed up for the event tonight, did you?"

"I guess I always look like a hillbilly. Is that what you're saying?"

I chuckled at his playful words. "Not really. It's just that you have the cowboy look going."

He shrugged again, his broad shoulders raising in the air before softening. "When you find something that works for you, you stick with it."

As a moment of silence fell, my thoughts wandered. After a few seconds of contemplation, I asked, "How are things going with Athena? Were you able to work anything out regarding the kids?"

He instantly sobered. "We had some pretty tough talks today. But we're trying to find a solution. I'll tell you what, I don't recommend divorce. It's hard."

I wondered what the inside scoop was on his divorce, but we weren't at the point where I could ask him that. However, he seemed remorseful over it, and I thought that was a good sign. At least he wasn't bashing his ex-wife like most people I knew who were divorced.

"By the way, I wanted to tell you that I ran into Langston earlier today."

My pulse quickened. "You did?"

"I did. I asked about what was going on."

"Did he share anything with you?" I couldn't help but think that Weston seemed entirely too calm right now to deliver any bad news.

"He said he's been selling some of the sound

equipment the school's been replacing. He said Devin has just been tossing it, and he saw the opportunity to make some money. He thought that's what you were there about."

"That's why he ran?"

Weston nodded. "That's what he said. I checked with Devin, who confirmed the facts about the old sound equipment. Langston was given a reprimand, but that's all the action that will be taken against him at this time."

"Good to know."

We pulled into the parking lot a few minutes later. In the distance, I saw that party lights had been strung between tree branches. White and orange balloons with music notes on them hung in the air.

A band played on the stage, and fun country-tinged music blared from the speakers. A dance floor stretched in the center of the festival area, and students moved with the music, almost like they didn't have a care in the world.

But I knew that wasn't true.

These kids were carrying far more burdens than they should at their age.

Weston and I glanced at each other, and I finally shrugged. "Here goes nothing, I guess."

He nodded. "Here goes nothing."

AS WESTON and I parted ways, I wove through the crowd and grabbed a glass of apple cider. I took a sip and let the cold liquid wash down my throat. I hadn't realized how dry my mouth was.

I paused beneath a willow tree and listened to everything around me. If I closed my eyes, I could hear the steamboat in the distance. I could hear the laughter in the crowd. And, of course, the music overwhelmed all the other sounds.

Beck and his band played some country tunes, and they were really good. The songs were catchy, well-written, and Beck's voice was easy on the ears.

Anyone looking in from the outside wouldn't guess the tragedies that happened here.

"This is how you dress like a hillbilly?"

I looked up and saw Mark White standing beside me wearing jeans and a flannel shirt. The look was totally different on him than it was on Weston.

Mark just looked out of place in his outfit, more like the type who belonged in polo shirts and khakis.

Phil would have been the same way.

"This is the best I could do." I glanced at my outfit and shrugged. Then I glanced back at the crowd. "It's good to see everybody having fun."

He turned to follow my gaze. "It is. It's been a tough week for them."

"How are you doing after the incident earlier?" I studied Mark's face, honestly wanting to know.

He raised a shoulder, but he wasn't fooling me. Natalie's death had shaken him up. Dead bodies tended to do that. For myself included. Every time I closed my eyes, I pictured Heather and Natalie. Somehow their faces always morphed into Scarlett's.

"I hate everything that's happened this week," he finally said. "That being said, I hope that we can put this all behind us. I think everybody does."

"That's for sure."

I sucked in a breath as two students walked in front of us carrying axes on their shoulders. What . . . ?

Mark touched my arm as if to break me from my fear. "Those axes aren't real. There are foam tips on them. We checked. Don't worry. No weapons are allowed."

I released my breath, realizing I'd probably over-reacted. But this week's events had me on edge more than I had thought. "Good to know."

As Mark stood beside me, he drew in a deep breath, and I heard something.

A slight wheeze.

Did he also have asthma?

Could he have been the person in my apartment? I didn't want to believe it. But I needed to keep my eyes wide open here.

"Well, it's great to see you, Camryn." Mark shifted. "You're definitely an asset here on campus, and I have a feeling you're just getting started."

I smiled and muttered, "Thank you," all the while wondering what that meant. Just getting started? Did that mean that my PR career here at the school hadn't even reached the climax of damage control I'd need to do?

I wasn't sure. But the statement was interesting.

As Mark walked away, my gaze went back to Beck. He was the next person on my suspect list, mostly because he was a front-runner as far as talent here at the school.

Now that I'd ruled out Langston, that left me with the front-runners who might be responsible for killing their competition.

Or Joseph.

I really didn't want to think of anyone here being responsible for the deaths.

CHAPTER TWENTY-SEVEN

AS THE BAND TOOK A BREAK, I watched Beck unstrap his guitar, set the instrument on a stand, and wander off the stage. Another student approached him, muttering something in low tones.

Even with my supersonic hearing, I couldn't pick up on what they said. Too many other noises floated around me. But I couldn't stop wondering if Beck was trying to eliminate the competition. It was the most likely motive I could think of.

I had to admit that, so far, my track record when it came to suspects wasn't great. The three people I'd initially suspected had been innocent. But it seemed I had plenty of other people in the queue.

Besides, I wasn't just a fixer. I considered myself a

finisher also. I hated leaving things undone, even if that was to my detriment.

As Beck headed away from the stage area, I set my apple cider on a table and tried to casually follow behind him. The good news was everyone was distracted with the festivities and no one seemed to notice me.

Beck rounded the corner, headed toward . . . the maintenance building?

Was there more to this whole side business Heather had going on than I'd initially thought? Was Beck somehow a part of this?

I didn't know, but I kept following.

The farther I headed from the festival area, the darker it became. Even though old-fashioned streetlights rose around me, they weren't as bright as I would have liked. Plus, all the crowds were back on Cobblestone Lawn.

As Beck glanced back, I sucked in a breath.

I needed to hide—now!

Quickly, I dashed behind a tree. As I pressed myself into the bark, my heart pounded in my ears with more intensity than I'd expected.

Had he seen me?

I wasn't sure.

But I *could* be following a killer, I reminded

myself. I had to be cautious.

I counted to three before peering out. Beck had started walking again. He wasn't looking at me.

I waited until he turned and disappeared behind the Grand Isle Cathedral.

His actions indicated he was up to something. He'd been glancing around, and his shoulders had looked tense.

I was determined to get to the bottom of this one way or another.

As soon as he was out of sight, I hurried back to the sidewalk and quietly headed after him. I didn't want to lose Beck. Probably nobody else could hear my steps, but I could. That fact made me paranoid. I kept glancing over my shoulder and looking into the shadows.

As soon as I turned the corner, something hard came down over my head.

Pain spread through my temples, and light flashed in front of me.

Then everything went black.

"CAMRYN? CAMRYN? ARE YOU OKAY?"

I pulled my eyes open and tried to focus my gaze.

Where was I? What happened? Who was talking to me?

I knew the answer to my last question. I knew whose voice that was.

Weston's.

I was . . . lying down? On the ground?

I blinked several times before trying to sit up.

Other voices sounded around me, concern masked in the fine tones. Footsteps scurried. But, mostly, I heard my heart pounding in my ears repeatedly.

Weston's arm snaked around my waist to help support me. That's when I felt the throbbing in my head again. Maybe that earlier feeling wasn't my heart after all.

Maybe it was my brain.

I blinked, wishing I could think more clearly. Wishing my vision wasn't blurry. Wishing I could shake this off. That didn't seem like a possibility.

"What happened?" I muttered.

"I don't know." Weston frowned as he examined me. "I rounded the corner and found you here. Your head . . . it's bleeding."

At once, everything rushed back to me. I'd been following Beck when something slammed into my head.

Why would Beck do that?

Unless he was hiding something.

"Somebody hit me," I finally said, realizing that Weston was waiting for an explanation.

Weston frowned. "That's what I gathered. Skittles called an ambulance and went to flag it down when it arrives."

I thought I'd just heard someone muttering "Turn around, don't drown" a few minutes ago. We'd be lucky if she came back with any help at all.

"I don't need an ambulance." I squeezed Weston's arm, trying to get through to him. "Please."

His lip twitched. "Then let me take you to the hospital to be checked out. You have a pretty nasty cut. I'm guessing you'll need some stitches."

I touched my forehead. When I pulled my hand away, I saw the blood on my fingertips.

Everything around me swam. I'd never been good with blood. Never.

As I saw other people stop in the distance to stare at me, I finally nodded at Weston. I didn't want to be any more of a spectacle than I already was.

"Fine," I told him. "We can go to the ER. But no ambulance."

"Okay, just give me a minute." He picked up his phone and made a few calls. Then he handed his keys to another student, muttered something to him, and the student took off—probably to pull up his truck.

After he slipped his phone back into his pocket, he reached to help me to my feet, keeping an arm around my waist. I wanted to argue that he didn't need to do that, but I was too unsteady on my feet to refuse.

He led me from the gawkers standing in the distance.

"Where are we going?" I asked. Were my words slurring? I couldn't be sure.

Thankfully, the closest street wasn't terribly far away because I wasn't sure I'd make it much further.

A student waited there, just as promised, standing beside Weston's truck. Weston helped me into the passenger's seat before handing me a spare T-shirt and pressing it against my head. The look of concern in his eyes touched me.

He was worried—just in a friendly way, I was sure.

Then he climbed into the driver's seat, and we took off down the road.

The nearest hospital wasn't that far away, yet it felt like it took years to get there.

I never thought I'd say I was glad that Weston had shown up. But I was.

Now I needed to find out who had done this to me.

CHAPTER TWENTY-EIGHT

AN HOUR LATER, I'd received six stitches to the top of my head and had been cleaned up. Detective Garrison had come and taken my statement. He'd said he would check some security footage, but we all knew that the cameras still hadn't been replaced. One of the parts was apparently backordered.

Garrison also said he'd question people at Trills and Thrills to see if anyone had seen anything. But the only one who could have possibly seen anything was Beck, and I doubted he'd admit to anything.

He'd moved up higher on my suspect list.

After I was finally cleared to leave the hospital, Weston helped me to my feet. He kept his hand on my arm as he led me from the building. He'd been a real godsend tonight.

When we stepped into the balmy air outside a few minutes later, he paused and turned to me. "You had me really worried there for a minute, you know."

I licked my lips as I remembered what happened. "I had myself pretty worried there for a minute. Thankfully, it all worked out."

He remained quiet a moment before finally asking, "Listen, I don't think you want to go back to Trills and Thrills, do you?"

I felt the throbbing in my head and frowned. That was the last place I wanted to be. "No, I don't."

He shrugged in an almost coy way. "I know this place that serves outstanding beignets. Would you like to try one?"

I should say no. I knew I should. But he had me at *beignet.*

"That might cheer me up a bit," I admitted.

Weston grinned and winked. "That's what I was hoping you'd say. Come on."

He led me to his truck, and we headed down the road, not making much conversation. I figured Weston was saving it for when we got to the restaurant.

Fifteen minutes later, he pulled up to a quaint little store in the riverfront area. *Bartholomew's* was written in blue neon letters across the top of the six-story, red-bricked building with various fire escapes snaking downward. Little café tables were in a fenced-in area at the front, and big picture windows showcased the restaurant inside.

Weston helped me from the truck and placed his hand on the small of my back as we headed toward the restaurant.

Somewhere not far away someone played a saxophone. Horse's hooves clacked against stone—a buggy ride, no doubt. A trolley car dinged.

The sounds made me feel right at home.

Then there were the scents. Fried pastries. The briny, slightly fishy aroma of the Savannah River. The scent of crisp leaves drying as autumn claimed them.

I paused in front of the restaurant and nodded approvingly. "It looks interesting."

"You're going to love it."

As soon as we stepped through the front door, a man and a woman behind the counter called hello to Weston. Just how many women had Weston brought here? Not that it mattered. This outing was purely platonic.

"Bart and Irma, this is my friend Camryn. Camryn, this is Bart and Irma."

I smiled and nodded, murmuring that it was nice to meet them.

"What can I get for you?" Bart nodded toward a display full of all kinds of pastries.

"One order of beignets with dark chocolate expresso sauce and one order of beignets with strawberry syrup and whipped topping," Weston said.

Those both sounded fantastic to me.

Weston and I settled at a corner table by the window where we could watch the river and all the people walking past. It was nearly ten o'clock, and I had no doubt this place would close soon. Several other people were here, leaning over iron-frame tables and speaking to each other in low tones.

I turned back to Weston. "How did you discover this place?"

"I like supporting local businesses. When I first came back to Grand Isle, I tried to find a new restaurant to eat at each week. This one has remained at the top of my favorites list."

"That's nice."

"I brought my niece Lizzie here, and she loved it."

My pulse quickened at the mention of his niece. "Lizzie? I haven't heard her name in years. How is she?"

Weston practically beamed. "She's great. She just started law school here in Savannah. Actually, she was out at Grand Isle just two nights ago."

Two nights ago? Two nights ago had been the candlelight vigil. The candlelight vigil where I'd seen Weston...

Realization hit me like a bucket of ice water. "*That* was Lizzie?"

He tilted his head as he glanced at me. "You saw her?"

"That couldn't be Lizzie. She's, like, three years old."

"She was . . . twenty years ago. She's now twenty-three." He paused and twisted his neck, his eyes never leaving me. "You didn't think Lizzie was . . ."

Dread filled my stomach when I realized where this conversation would go. "Your girlfriend? Maybe."

He pressed his lips together before twisting his head as if my statement had been hard to stomach. "Apparently, you think I like younger women."

I shrugged, knowing there was no need to deny it. "Most men in the business do."

"I didn't think you'd be jaded."

Jaded? It wasn't what people usually called me.

"Generally, I'm not. But . . ." I didn't know how to finish my statement.

He observed me, something unreadable lingering in his gaze. Finally, he said, "I'm not the man you think I am."

I felt my cheeks heat. "How do you know who I think you are?"

"Intuition."

I felt my cheeks warm even more. Thankfully, before I had to provide a comeback, our food was delivered.

Because this was one public relations situation I didn't know how to get myself out of.

I TOOK the last bite of my beignet and wiped my mouth with a paper napkin. "That was delicious."

Weston grinned. "I thought that you might like it. It's some of the best, right?"

"I definitely want to come back here. However, for the sake of my waistline, I will need to pace myself."

"Nothing wrong with that." He dropped a few dollars on the table as a tip and then stood, offering his hand to help me up.

I slipped my fingers in the palm of his hand and stood beside him. Just as quickly, I pulled my arm back to my side and kept a composed look on my face.

Touching Weston was *not* something I wanted to do.

Yet, it was.

Which was exactly why I shouldn't do it.

Weston nodded toward the river in the distance. "How do you feel about walking down the waterfront for a few minutes to burn off some of those calories? It's a nice evening outside and—"

"That sounds wonderful."

Walking up and down this area had been a favorite activity of mine and Weston's back in college. In fact, when we had both been freshmen, we'd decided to come out here with Weston's guitar. We'd open the case and sing duets together and watch as people threw money into the case. One day, we made almost three hundred dollars and thought we were rich. We'd even gone out to dinner together to celebrate.

I smiled at the memory.

"This is a great area, isn't it?" Weston slowly strolled beside me on the sidewalk.

I crossed my arms over my chest, reminding

myself not to touch him again. As I shivered, Weston took off his leather jacket and draped it over my shoulders.

At once, his scent filled my nostrils. Leather. Evergreen. Hints of the beignets.

I shoved those thoughts aside so I could focus on the environment around me.

I loved everything about this area. I even tried to talk Phil into moving here one time when he was talking about relocating his headquarters for his business. I couldn't convince him. Apparently, Savannah wasn't central enough.

"I'm glad you're back here now, Camryn—despite the circumstances that have brought you here." Weston's voice rumbled with sincerity.

Weston didn't need to spell it out. Those circumstances included a lot of death. Not just Phil's, but now three students on campus.

I frowned at the thought before remembering Weston had started his statement with a compliment. "Thank you."

"Can I ask you a question?" Weston asked after a moment.

As soon as his words hit my ears, my spine tightened. That question was always a sign that whatever the inquiry was wouldn't be pleasant.

"You can ask," I finally said. "I'm just not promising to answer."

He grinned again. "Fair enough. You don't have a car here, do you?"

My throat constricted. "I don't."

"Why not?"

I drew in a deep breath, wondering how much I wanted to share. But then I remembered that there was no shame in struggling. That's what my therapist always told me.

"I don't drive anymore," I admitted.

His grin slipped as he glanced at me, the moonlight catching his eyes and bathing his face in a pleasant pale yellow. "Why not?"

Memories tried to assault me, but I pushed them back. I couldn't tell Weston why without delving into the pain of my past.

Part of me didn't want to. Another part of me thought opening up might be healthy.

I licked my lips, not sure what words would leave my lips—denial or the truth.

"I was driving the night that Phil was killed." My voice sounded scratchy, even to my own ears. My subconscious had clearly pushed out the truth—probably a good choice.

But not every truth was meant to be shared with

every person. Privacy was still a basic right.

Realization flooded Weston's gaze as he seemed to process my words. "Oh, Camryn . . ."

"It doesn't seem fair that I survived and Phil didn't." That fact constantly haunted me, nearly feeling like a companion at times—an unwanted but deserved companion.

Weston gently squeezed my arm. "I'm sorry. I shouldn't have asked."

I rubbed my bicep, suddenly feeling chilled even with his jacket draped over me. "It's okay. It's . . . it's all part of my history now."

"I heard a drunk driver hit you."

Memories of that evening continued to pummel me. If I let myself, I'd drift back in time. Drift back to the conversation Phil and I had been having only seconds before everything changed.

We'd been talking about fried pickles, of all things.

Fried pickles.

"A drunk driver did hit us," I finally said. "Everyone always tells me the accident wasn't my fault and that I can't blame myself. Yet I can't stop doing just that. If I'd just gone a little faster or slower or if I'd glanced to the left before going through that intersection . . ." My voice cracked.

"Camryn..."

I wasn't done yet. "The what-ifs can tear a person apart inside. I didn't want to get back in a car for a long time, but I finally forced myself. Even after months of therapy, I haven't been able to force myself to get behind the wheel."

"I'm sure it's normal, that it's going to take time."

"Maybe." As I said the word, a new somberness hung in the air.

What else was there to say?

Nothing.

But nothing could change what had happened.

"Do you want to talk about it more?" Weston asked.

I shook my head. "Not really."

"How about if I drive you home then."

"Please."

Without another word, we started back to his truck.

Sharing had made me feel raw and vulnerable. I wanted to take my words back.

But now Weston knew the truth. My secrets couldn't be held against me or used as a weapon.

Because too many times, that was exactly what happened.

CHAPTER TWENTY-NINE

"I KNOW I'm going to regret asking this." Weston had started his truck, but we remained in the parking lot unmoving. "What do you think is going on at the campus? I know I told you that you shouldn't get involved, and I know that you've gotten involved anyway. Clearly, someone is trying to hide something. Otherwise, this person wouldn't have gone after you."

A pulse of excitement quickened my heartbeat.

Weston had *actually* asked. Had *actually* wanted to talk about this.

And I desperately wanted someone to bounce my ideas off. Why not Weston?

"I'm not a hundred percent sure what's going on, but I keep going back to the front-runners in the talent competition. I know this might sound crazy, but what if someone's trying to kill off the competition?"

Weston frowned before shaking his head. "I know most of the front-runners, and I have trouble thinking that any of them did this."

The problem was, Weston didn't know what I knew. "I was following Beck tonight. I walked around the corner after him. The next thing I knew, someone hit me over the head."

Weston's eyes widened. "Do you think Beck did it?"

"I have no idea, but he makes the most sense." I didn't want to throw out accusations. They could ruin a person. I knew about that. But I was just speaking the truth.

Weston stared off in space a moment before shaking his head again. "I just can't see it."

"Joseph said someone tried to sabotage the competition a few years ago. Who's to say that's not happening again? Look what's at stake . . ."

"I agree there's a lot at stake. But . . ." Weston ran a hand over his face. "I just don't know. When someone tried to sabotage it before there were mishaps with sound equipment and the auditorium got flooded. But it was nothing dangerous."

"Let me turn the tables for a moment. If you had to guess, who do you think might be responsible for something like this?"

His eyes widened as if in surprise. "I don't know. I've been thinking about it a lot. Thinking about why somebody might want to kill the students. I haven't come up with any good ideas."

"How about any bad ideas?"

He let out a chuckle. "No bad ideas either. I guess I don't want to think about people at the school being that cutthroat. Maybe part of me hopes that whoever is behind it isn't a part of our school."

"It would be really hard for a stranger to get on campus and do all of this, though."

"I agree."

I turned to him, more questions lingering in my head. "I heard that Heather was a part of some type of secret society. Do you know anything about that?"

His eyes widened and his breath caught. "Secret society?"

"That's what I heard."

He ran his hand across the steering wheel and glanced out the windshield. "I don't know what to tell you."

My human lie detector was beeping loudly. "I think you do."

"I have been sworn to silence."

My pulse quickened. Weston knew something. So why wasn't he sharing? Why would he want to hide it?

Unless he was guilty.

Was that the truth? Was he somehow complicit in what had happened?

I didn't want to think it was the truth. But I'd be a fool not to consider every possibility.

WESTON LET out a sigh and stared straight ahead, the truck still not moving.

"A few of the students last year started what was called the Sweet Tea and Forgotten Composer Society. I think they got the idea just from movies and books, and then they romanticized it. Heather was a part of it. She decided along with five of her friends to meet every week at a secret location—"

"A secret location?"

"It's actually in the basement of the library. They all meet to talk about their favorite songs, writers, movies, and books. They bring sweet tea to drink. Sometimes they wear oversized floppy hats just to feel fancy. It's really simple and innocent."

"If it's so simple and innocent, why the secrets?"

Weston shrugged, still nonchalant. "Because it's a secret society. If everybody knew about it, it wouldn't be a secret anymore."

"But we're talking about murders here. I can understand in the general sense of things why you wouldn't share. But in light of what happened . . ."

Weston's face twitched as if he didn't like where I was going with this. "If you must know, Hannon banned any secret societies. He made it clear if anyone was found participating in them, they'd be forced to leave the school."

That seemed like an overreaction. There had to be more to this story. "What? What's the big deal?"

"Another secret society several years ago started harassing other students—bullying them. It caused a lot of emotional turmoil. But not every secret society is like that. I thought he had a knee-jerk reaction and that his decree was over the top."

I stored the new information in the back of my mind.

"Was that why the two of you were talking? You and Heather?"

He narrowed his eyes. "You know about that?"

I nodded.

"Yes, that's why. Heather asked me what I

thought about it, and I told her to go for it. I thought Joseph's rule was too strict."

"Why did Garrison meet with you?" The question left my lips before I could stop it.

Weston let out a long breath. "Heather's phone showed that she called me right before she did her sound check for the talent show. He wanted to ask me what it was about."

"And?"

"You're pushy, aren't you?" An unreadable emotion flickered in his gaze. "It's like I told Detective Garrison—she called about the secret society. Wanted to know if she could get thrown out of school for being a part of one. I told her I didn't think so. Still, I know how it looks when a student calls a faculty member. I didn't want to make a big deal of it."

"I see." I supposed all that made sense.

Weston appeared to be done with this conversation because he started down the dark road snaking in front of us.

A backroad led to the campus, and that was the direction we headed.

I was still mulling over what Weston had said when I noticed him glance into the rearview mirror and tense.

Without asking any questions, I looked behind us and saw headlights there. When I glanced back at Weston, I knew by the set of his eyes that he was getting nervous. That car behind us was driving close. Too close.

"Weston . . . ?"

"I'm just being cautious." But the tension in his voice said otherwise.

I glanced behind us again in time to notice the headlights were gone. Not because the car disappeared.

But because it was so close that we could no longer see them.

My lungs tensed as I turned around.

Somebody was following us. Or was it more than merely following us?

As if to answer my question, the other vehicle nudged Weston's truck.

Instantly, my thoughts went into a tailspin. My mind went back to the night of the accident. The night Phil had died because of a drunk driver.

I could hardly control my breathing. Panic flooded through me as I remembered the screeching of brakes. The crunching of metal. The terrified scream that emerged from my lungs.

Then there had been a whoosh as the airbags

deployed. The sickening silence in the immediate aftermath of the tragedy. Finally, the urgent murmurs of bystanders as they'd stopped to help.

I pressed my ears, wishing I could erase the memories. Wishing the sounds didn't seem so real.

But I was at the mercy of the auditory memories pummeling me.

Weston pressed the accelerator, and we hurried down the road at a fast clip.

But, as I glanced behind me once more, the headlights remained too close. The car quickly accelerated toward us.

As it did, Weston hit a slick patch.

The next thing I knew, we careened off the road, headed right toward a tree.

CHAPTER THIRTY

WESTON'S TRUCK stopped only inches from colliding with the tree.

As it did, I heard the squeal of tires behind us.

The car sped away: mission accomplished.

My heart pounded out of control and shakes overtook my whole body. My limbs felt cold. My head swam.

"Camryn?"

Flashbacks pummeled me. Beat me. Haunted me.

Phil...

Tears rushed to my eyes as I thought about our accident. When I remembered glancing in the passenger seat. When I visualized his lifeless body—

"Camryn?" a deep voice said.

Phil's image remained in my mind.

Two hands grasped my shoulders and shook me slightly, snapping me out of my stupor.

It wasn't Phil, though.

It was . . . Weston.

"Camryn? Are you okay?"

His face slowly came into focus.

I was with Weston. In his truck.

Phil was gone.

Nothing would change that.

Ever.

A cry escaped from somewhere deep inside me.

"I need to know that you're okay . . ." Weston's voice sounded demanding but calm.

Weston.

Phil.

My mind volleyed back and forth between their images until everything spun around me.

I was with Weston right now. We'd almost hit a tree.

But we were alive.

"Are you okay?" Weston said the words slowly, precisely.

I heard the worry there. His tone was near panic.

Finally, I forced myself to nod. "I'm . . . okay."

His face fell with relief, and he let out a breath. "I need to call the police."

I nodded again, wishing I didn't feel so cold. But I did. I was freezing.

It was shock, I realized. I was lucid enough to grasp that.

A few seconds later, Weston put his phone away and turned back to me. "You're scaring me, Camryn."

I had to snap out of this. What would my therapist tell me?

Focus on what you can control.

What *could* I control right now? My thoughts?

They felt like they had a mind of their own.

Images of the night Phil died just kept replaying in my head again and again, no matter how hard I tried to stop them.

Moisture spilled down my cheeks.

"Camryn . . ." Weston said my name softly.

The next instant, he unhooked my seatbelt and pulled me into his arms.

Normally, I might resist. But right now, I welcomed the comfort he offered.

He folded me into him, and I rested my head on his shoulder as tears poured from my eyes. How had my life been turned upside down like this?

It wasn't supposed to be this way. I'd tried to make the best of it, but for what purpose? I'd never get Phil back and . . .

"It's going to be okay . . ." Weston murmured in my ear.

But nothing felt like it would be okay. Not ever again.

GARRISON MET Weston and me on the highway to take our statements. We'd remained there in case he needed to compare tire treads or for any other reason.

My mind still felt scattered, and the trembles hadn't left me yet. Weston remained at my side as if afraid I might pass out.

Garrison had come alone this time. "Did you get a look at the vehicle's license plate?"

Weston shook his head. "Everything happened too fast."

Garrison's gaze fell on me again. "You think this is related to the break-in at your place last night?"

Weston stiffened beside me. "Someone broke into your place? Again?"

I shrugged. "I was going to mention that, but . . ."

Not that I was obligated to mention it to anyone. But right now, I felt like I should have.

"Cam . . ." Weston stared at me.

He really needed to stop saying my name.

Sure, we'd shared a moment. But that didn't mean anything in the grand scheme of things.

We might have a past together, but that didn't mean we had a future.

"I'm glad you two are okay." Garrison slid his notepad back into the pocket of his jacket. "We'll keep our eyes open. Maybe someone somewhere saw something."

"They didn't," I told him before shrugging. "I know that sounds pessimistic, but I'm sure that's the case. That's the way this whole investigation has gone, isn't it?"

Garrison frowned. "I want to argue with you, but I can't. You're right."

"Wait . . . you're saying you think there's more to this also?" Weston stared at Garrison.

The detective nodded. "I do. The deaths of the students on campus haven't officially been reopened as homicides, but I'm doing some investigating behind the scenes."

Weston shook his head. "This just gets worse and worse. The talent show is tomorrow night."

"We know. We have no reason to believe any of the students participating will be in danger."

"But you don't know that." Weston stared at him.

Garrison frowned. "No, we don't."

A few minutes later, Garrison was gone, leaving Weston and me standing there. As Weston turned back toward me, I felt my heart give an involuntary flutter.

"Are you sure you're okay?" Weston asked. "I hate to keep asking you that, but . . ."

"I'm fine," I rushed. "Thank you for all your help. I really appreciate it."

He stared at me another moment, something crackling between us.

Chemistry.

It had always been there, and it was still there now.

But that didn't mean anything.

I forced myself to look away. "I should probably get home."

He stared at me another moment before nodding. "Let's go."

CHAPTER THIRTY-ONE

THE NEXT MORNING, I was back in my office. Everything at the school centered around talent show preparations. The show would start at 5:30, and it would be a hustle to get things ready in time.

Weston had driven me home last night and had insisted on checking out my place.

Everything was clear, so he'd reluctantly left.

It was better that way. I needed space from him, even if I *had* had a nice outing with him after my injury and he'd been nothing but a gentleman.

I frowned as I sat at my desk and drank some coffee before diving into my to-do list. I didn't know why, but I had a bad feeling in my gut today.

Someone knocked at my door, and I glanced up

and saw Weston there. He stepped closer, not fully coming inside. "You doing okay today?"

I nodded, suspicion still hounding me, all based on the way he stood. "I am. Thank you."

"Good. I found somebody who wants to talk to you."

"Someone who wants to talk to *me*?" A spike of excitement flittered inside me. What did Weston know that I didn't?

A second later, Beck Tarsus appeared beside Weston. The student offered an apologetic smile as he took a step closer.

"I heard what happened last night, and I'm sorry," he said. "But I want you to know that I didn't attack you. I didn't even know you were behind me or that anything happened until late last night."

I wanted to believe him. I really did. But I needed more information first. "Where did you run off to after your set was over?"

He let out a breath before frowning. "I've been getting these threatening text messages. Whoever is sending them said if I don't drop out of the talent show that something bad will happen to Lindsey, my girlfriend."

Alarm raced through me. "What? Did these messages start before or after your accident?"

"After. Part of me wonders if that accident was intended to do more than just shake me up." Beck frowned again and rubbed his neck as if his muscles were suddenly tight.

My thoughts continued to race. "Did you ever hear what the cause of the accident was?"

"My car lost brake fluid and I couldn't slow down as I was rounding a corner. Thankfully, nobody else was there for my car to collide into."

He was right. Things could have turned out a lot differently. "You were lucky."

He nodded, even though his eyes still looked dull with worry. "Yes, ma'am. I was."

I let out a breath and I tried to form a mental timeline of what had happened. "So, you started getting the threats afterward. Was anything specific mentioned other than Lindsey?"

"The second text hinted that she might disappear, never to be found again."

My pulse quickened. "How many threatening messages did you get?"

"As of last night, three."

"Did anything else happen? Did this person carry through with his threats?"

"The message I got last night said that they had Lindsey and were holding her in my dorm room.

That I had five minutes to get there." Beck's voice broke.

"She wasn't at Trills and Thrills?"

"She was, but then I couldn't find her. It turns out, someone locked her in the bathroom, but she was fine. I think someone just wanted to let me know they were serious."

"Why didn't you mention this earlier?" I asked.

Beck's gaze darkened. "The sender said if I told anybody about the threats then something bad would happen."

That sounded about par for the course.

My thoughts continued to race. "Did you go to the police with this yet?"

"After I heard what happened to you, I talked to them this morning. Professor Turner went with me."

I looked over at Weston and nodded, hoping the gratitude showed in my eyes. "Thank you. I appreciate the update."

Beck nodded. "Of course. I hope whoever is doing all this is put behind bars. In the meantime, I'm not one to be intimidated. The only thing I worry about is Lindsey . . ."

After he left, Weston remained in my office, still staring at me, an ocean of thought crashing and receding in his gaze.

What exactly was he thinking right now? "Why are you looking at me like that?"

His eyes remained on me, saying far more than his words would. "I hardly got any sleep last night. I was too worried about you."

"As you can see, I'm fine." I raised my hands as if to prove it.

"I'm glad. But I have a request."

I crossed my arms and leaned back in my chair. "Shoot."

"If you're going to follow anyone as you're chasing down any leads, could you let me know first? If not me, then someone else? I just hate to think about something else happening to you." His tone held sincerity and worry.

Warmth flooded my heart when I realized how good it felt to have someone watching out for me. "I appreciate that. I'll do my best to inform you before I do anything stupid."

"Good." He took a step back, his sinewy muscles pulling beneath his chambray shirt. "I've got to go help with setup for the show tonight. You're going to be there?"

"I have a few more things to do here in the office first. But I'll see you at Hannon Auditorium."

"That sounds good." He opened his mouth as if

he was about to say more then paused and waved instead. "I'll see you around, Cam."

As he left, I crossed Beck Tarsus off my list.

Thus-said list was getting smaller and smaller.

However, it still wasn't small enough for my comfort.

CHAPTER THIRTY-TWO

I HAD to take several more phone calls from parents who wanted to pull their kids out of Grand Isle. I knew these weren't empty threats. If something didn't change on campus soon, this whole place could be shut down.

Was that what someone wanted? Did the person behind these crimes hate the school so much that he wanted to see it fail? Had that been the motive this whole time?

I didn't know.

My phone rang, and I saw it was Scarlett. Everything else was forgotten as I answered. "Hey, you. What's going on?"

"Sorry to call you in the middle of the day, but I wanted to give you an update. That guy that I thought was stalking me? He's actually on the student newspaper, and he was trying to get up the nerve to ask me for an update on your career."

"On me?"

"Yes, Mom. Some people still think you're a big deal."

I chuckled. "Good to know."

"Anyway, he's totally not a threat, and I thought you'd want to know."

"Thanks for the update. Did you give him a quote?"

"As Dad would say: No way, no chance, no how. Family is private."

I felt pride beam inside me. "Good girl."

"I've gotta run, Mom. But we'll talk again later. I love you."

"I love you too." I smiled as I lowered my phone. At least, that was one less thing I had to worry about.

I stood and stretched, heading out to take a walk and get some fresh air to clear my head.

But as soon as I stepped out of the administration wing, I heard singing down the hallway. I recognized the voice.

It was Anita, the housekeeper.

As I rounded the corner, I spotted her mopping

the floor. Today, she sang "I Wanna Dance with Somebody" but she substituted "clean" for "dance."

I smiled at the joy in her voice.

"If it isn't Camryn Paine." Anita greeted me with a grin that quickly faded. "So sorry to hear about what happened to you last night."

I paused near her. Apparently, word had spread around campus pretty quickly. "Thank you. I appreciate it."

She stopped mopping and took another step closer to me. "I heard that happened to you because you're looking into the students who mysteriously died here on campus. Is that right?"

My throat tightened at her words. "That theory makes the most sense."

She lowered her voice even more. "Do you have any leads?"

I shrugged, smart enough not to go around accusing people. "I'm not at liberty to say."

She glanced around again before leaning closer. "I know I shouldn't say this but . . . I was cleaning the administrative wing late last night. It's not something I normally do, but we're down two workers, so I'm having to pick up extra shifts."

"Did something happen?" The way she spoke to

me, as if sharing a secret, made my hope surge that she might have something useful to share.

"I can't say something really happened. But when I was outside Joseph Hannon's door . . ." She paused and pressed her lips together, her eyes flickering with indecision.

My breath caught when I realized she was on the verge of saying something potentially important. "Did you see or hear something?"

"I overheard Hannon on the phone in his office. Your name came up."

My heart beat harder. "What did he say?"

"He said that the board pressured him to hire you, but that he thought it was a mistake."

Her words felt like a slap in the face. "Is that right?"

I tried to remain composed so that it wouldn't show how much her words had shaken me.

"I thought it was weird to hear him say that behind closed doors since he always says such glowing things about you in public," Anita continued. "I don't know if his conversation has anything to do with what's happening here. But did you ever think that maybe he didn't realize you were as good at your job as you are? Maybe *he's* the one who wants to get rid of you?"

My lungs tightened at her words. "I never thought of that. But I appreciate you letting me know."

Anita stepped back and frowned, moisture pooling in her eyes. "I like to think of all the students as my own. I can't stand what's happening to them. I hope I didn't overstep by sharing this with you. Please, don't tell anyone you got this information from me. I can't afford to lose my job, especially not with a daughter in college."

"I understand. I'll keep this between us."

But as I continued down the hallway, Anita's words turned over in my mind.

I'd already considered Joseph as a suspect. But if he was the one behind this, why did he hire me?

Unless what Anita said was true. Unless the board members had pressured Joseph and he had no other choice. Then, when he figured out that I was getting closer to the answers, maybe he'd tried to silence me.

I shivered. I didn't like the thought of that.

But maybe it was something I needed to consider a little bit more.

BY THE TIME I got back to my office, a new theory lingered in my head. The faces of all the people I'd suspected might be guilty ran through my mind, as well as possible motives, means, and opportunities.

I'd ruled out a lot of people. But I was certain that whoever was behind these murders was someone affiliated with the school.

They'd known about the talent show sound check. They'd known the order of performers. They'd known Heather had a peanut allergy. They'd known who the top contenders were.

I quickly did some research on my computer, and I stopped at one name.

The name of the person who was now my prime suspect.

Everything fit. The motive, means, and opportunity.

I couldn't believe I hadn't seen this before.

But now I had to prove it.

I glanced at the time.

The show started in five minutes. I had to get to Hannon Auditorium.

Quickly, I called Garrison so I could share my theory. He didn't answer.

I tried again, and he still didn't answer.

The third time, I left him a message. If I was onto something, he needed to know.

Jamming my phone back into my pocket, I hurried across the campus. As I did, I kept my eyes open for my new number one suspect. How could I have not seen this before? But my theory made sense.

The person who'd staged these murders needed to be put behind bars.

I stepped into the back of the auditorium just as Jinky walked onstage. She was acting as emcee for the event. Her glimmering royal-blue dress and the tiara on her head totally fit her personality.

"To say I'm just obsessed with this talent show would be an understatement," she started.

I smiled. Jinky loved being obsessed with things.

Weston stood near the door and glanced over at me as soon as I slipped inside. I felt his eyes on me— and the questions there. *Was I okay? Had anything else happened?*

I offered a smile, trying to reassure him.

Then I looked around for my number one suspect.

This person was here and would strike again. I felt certain of it.

It was just a matter of when.

CHAPTER THIRTY-THREE

HALFWAY THROUGH THE TALENT SHOW, everything was running on tempo. I almost couldn't believe it.

Weston had remained in the back of the auditorium with me, probably not because he had been assigned to the area but because he wanted to keep an eye on me. I supposed that was sweet, even if it was also unnecessary.

But as a female got up to sing, one of the stagehands found Weston and nodded toward the back of the stage.

I knew that meant they needed Weston's help backstage.

Before leaving, Weston stepped closer to me and lowered his voice. "I need to go help with an in-ear monitor issue. Are you going to be okay here by yourself?"

"Of course." The words rolled off my tongue a little too easily.

He stared at me another moment, and I knew exactly what he was thinking. Beck was supposed to go onstage.

One more act, and it was his turn. I felt like if anybody was going to be targeted tonight, it would be Beck.

Weston slipped out the back door and disappeared from sight. As he did, I crossed my arms and leaned against the wall so I could listen. And when I said listen, I meant not only to the performers but to everything else around me as well.

I heard the occasional whisper in the audience. Someone dropped a pen. Someone accidentally plucked a guitar string backstage.

One other sound caught my ear.

I closed my eyes, trying to focus on what I'd heard and to mute everything else.

I'd worked hard to perfect the skill over the years, but, when I tried hard enough, I could usually do it.

What was that? A new sound was *definitely* coming from the stage area.

Come on, Camryn . . .

I heard it again. Clearly, no one else did. Whatever the noise was, it blended in with everything else. And it was faint.

I paused as the sound hit my ears again. It was a squeak.

It almost sounded like it came from . . . the catwalk.

My breath caught as I realized what was probably about to happen.

Wasting no more time, I stepped out the back door.

I had to get to the catwalk and stop the killer before someone else was hurt.

I KNEW I should tell Weston what I'd heard. I'd pretty much promised him I would. But right now, I didn't have any time to lose.

As I ran toward the backstage area, I knew there were no guarantees I'd run into Weston there. But I hoped that might be the case.

My hands trembled as I pulled out my phone and dialed his number.

He didn't answer.

No doubt he'd put his phone on silent. It was what a responsible adult would do in the middle of a talent show. But that didn't help me now.

I reached the backstage and threw the door open. As I glanced around at the stagehands, none of them were paying attention to me or to the catwalk.

I searched the faces there. Where was Weston? I thought he was coming back here, but I didn't see him now. Maybe I'd misunderstood.

I spotted Langston and dashed toward him. As he heard me approaching, he looked up at me and his eyes widened as if he were startled.

I didn't have time to put him at ease. Instead, I rushed, "Have you seen Weston?"

"Weston? No. I don't know where he is."

"How do you get to the top of the catwalk?" I nodded at the metal walkway above me.

"You have to go through that closet door. Why?"

I followed his gaze and saw the door was closed with no one around it. "Have you seen anyone go up there recently?"

"No. No one should be up there now. The lighting is already set."

But as I glanced up, I felt certain I saw a shadow moving above the stage area.

I could think of only one other thing to do other than screaming for everyone to get off the stage.

I needed to go up there and check things out myself.

I pushed past Langston and opened the closet door. Before anyone could stop me, I began to climb.

Heights weren't my favorite thing, but I was going to have to conquer them now.

I'd had to walk on a catwalk one time during a show and then be lowered by a wire for one of my songs. Thoughts of that moment still caused a shot of terror to rush through me.

I pushed the memories aside.

I wondered if my number one suspect was up here on the catwalk. Was my theory right? Had Garrison gotten my message?

I wasn't sure. But as I reached the top of the ladder, a jolt of fear went through me. I had to push past it. I had to do this.

I gripped the rails and pulled myself up. As I stood on the catwalk, I felt my head swirling.

I could do this. I had no choice.

I stared straight ahead of me but didn't see anybody. Someone had been up here. Had this person been tampering with one of the lights? That was my best guess.

I had only a few minutes to figure this out. If I couldn't, I was going to have to make a spectacle of myself in order to shut this down and get everyone off the stage. It was the only choice I had.

Just as that thought crossed my head, I looked down and saw Jinky stride onstage. The next act she announced?

Beck Tarsus.

My breath caught. I didn't have any time to waste.

I started across the catwalk, looking for the person who'd been up here.

But just as Beck walked onstage to the applause of the crowd, something crashed below me.

A spotlight.

Somebody *had* been up here messing with it.

And I had to find this person. Now.

CHAPTER THIRTY-FOUR

SCREAMS ECHOED IN THE AUDIENCE. Beneath me, people scrambled from the stage.

Weston had tackled Beck right before the light hit him, and right now they both lay sprawled on stage.

As I glanced down, I saw Weston stare up. He frowned before muttering, "Cam?"

I had no time to explain. The person up here could try to get away.

From what I remembered, there were only two ways to get on and off this catwalk. If I listened closely, I could hear footsteps running in the opposite direction.

"Wait!" I wasn't sure why I yelled the word as if I expected this person to listen.

I suppose it had been instinct. Either way, I took off in a run. If I stared straight ahead and not down, I didn't feel dizzy.

The shadow headed toward the area of the catwalk that stretched above the audience.

Oh no . . . not the audience. Not that way.

Why couldn't this Shadow Person simply have scrambled down and run out of the building?

I knew why. Because they would be too easy to catch that way. There was a better chance of getting away up here on this catwalk.

I tried to remember just how far this metal plank stretched. Did the walkway extend all the way back to the sound booth?

It might. If my memory served me correctly, that was *exactly* where the platform led.

As I started to step onto another area leading even higher than the one above the stage, I glanced down at the panicked crowds as they scrambled from the building.

My head swam when I realized how high I was. I hated heights. *Hated* them.

But as I saw the shadow disappearing, I knew I had to keep going.

My phone rang in my pocket, and my gut told me it was probably Weston. Maybe Garrison. I wasn't sure. But there was no way that I could keep running *and* answer it *and* remain on this platform.

But whoever was calling tried again.

I paused, grabbed the phone from my pocket, and put it up to my ear.

"Cam, what are you doing?" It was Weston.

I glanced ahead. "The person who did this . . . they're up here."

"Come down. Let the police get them."

"I can't. I can't let them get away."

"Cam . . . where are you now?" Exasperation and worry clashed in his voice.

I stared at the narrow stretch in front of me that led to the back of the auditorium. "I'm headed toward the sound booth."

"You can't go that way."

"Why not?" Was Weston simply determined to tell me what to do?

"Because the catwalk ends before you reach that area. It's being repaired. All the sound techs and crew know that. You need to get down. Now."

As I gripped the phone, I glanced below me again. My head spun, and I let out a gasp.

The phone slipped through my fingers and cascaded below. It hit the floor and shattered.

No . . .

Fear paralyzed me for a moment. My one means of talking to people was now gone.

Then I looked up and saw Shadow Person had stepped toward me.

The perpetrator must have realized the catwalk ended. Now the killer was coming back this way.

I had to figure out exactly what I was going to do about it.

"YOU SHOULD HAVE LEFT THINGS ALONE," Shadow Person growled, clearly using some type of voice modulator that made their tone sound almost robotic.

I knew there were certain types you could strap around your throat, almost like a choker necklace. I could only assume this person was using one of those now.

I stepped back, pondering if I could turn and run without falling to my death.

I wasn't sure.

"You tried to kill Beck tonight," I muttered. "Did you really think you were going to get away with it?"

I took another step back.

My mind raced. Even if the police were able to

get up here, how were they going to help me? They couldn't exactly put themselves between me and the killer.

Those were things I should have thought about.

Shadow Person kept creeping closer and closer, almost as if they had no fear. Why? Had this person given up? Did they figure that they were in no hurry now because certainly they'd be caught?

That wouldn't bode well for me.

I continued creeping back, my hands on the railing just in case I slipped.

As the thought crossed my mind, my foot hit the edge of the catwalk, and I felt myself tumbling. I gasped and caught myself.

People below screamed.

Could they see me? Was Weston down there watching also?

"I had a plan, and you messed it all up," Shadow Person hissed. "I thought it would scare you off, but it didn't work."

"I'm very persistent. I have a bit of an obsession with finishing projects once I start them."

"You should have stopped."

Hands still on the rails, I crept back and back and back. But for every step I took, I felt like Shadow Person took three steps closer.

What would the killer do upon reaching me? Push me to my death? Strangle me?

I didn't know, and I didn't really want to think about it.

"Do you know what I do to people who ruin my plans?" Shadow Person hissed.

My blood ran cooler at the question. "No, what?"

"I kill them."

My throat tightened. That was what I feared the person might say.

I took another step back. This time my foot hit one of the steps leading from the catwalk above the audience to the catwalk above the stage.

I started to stumble again, my weight and momentum pulling me down. The only thing keeping me upright was my grip on the railing.

"There's no need to stop yourself," the killer said. "Make it easy for me. Fall to your death simply because you're clumsy."

Resolve hardened in me. No way would I make this easy. "That's not going to happen."

"Fine. Let's do this the hard way." The killer grabbed something from their waist.

A knife.

I sucked in a breath at the sight of the blade.

As I continued to stare at it, footsteps pounded toward me from behind.

"Cam, come to me." I knew whose voice it was. Weston's. "You can do it."

Oh, Weston . . . you shouldn't have inserted yourself into the middle of this. I can't let two people die because of my actions.

"I see Romeo is coming to save you," Shadow Person said. "It's not going to work."

Shadow Person stepped closer and reached for the mask. But before stripping it off, I knew whose face I'd see on the other side.

As the mask came off, my theory was confirmed.

Anita Anderson was behind all of this.

CHAPTER THIRTY-FIVE

"ANITA, it's not too late to make this right." I knew I probably couldn't talk any sense into her, but I had to try.

She shook her head, all signs of the cheerful woman I'd previously met gone.

"It's too late for that." Her voice came out digitalized again. As if realizing she still wore the voice modulator, she ripped it off her neck and sneered. "I know how it ends for me. But you're the one who ruined all of this. You ruined my plan."

"I know why you're doing this," I continued. "Your daughter applied to Grand Isle, but she wasn't accepted. She's on the waiting list to get in. You thought if you killed off a few key students then maybe a spot would open up for her."

Anita's gaze darkened as she still gripped the knife. "How'd you know?"

"I decided to check the waiting list, and I saw your daughter's name. Everything suddenly made sense. *You* made sense."

The woman continued to sneer. "Annabelle is so talented. She deserves to be here."

"I'm sure she wouldn't want you killing people to make that happen. She could have auditioned again next year."

"You don't understand." Anita's voice rose. "I can't let her throw her life away and be like me. I always wanted to be a singer, but I never pursued it. Now look at me. I'm cleaning a college campus. I can't let that be her life."

"Just because she didn't get in at Grand Isle doesn't mean that will be her life."

"I can't let her follow in my footsteps." Anita sucked in a labored breath, a wheeze whistling through her windpipe.

Asthma, I realized. I'd heard that sound before—when my purse was stolen. And Anita's stout figure that could easily look masculine with the right clothing and shadows.

"Right now, following in your footsteps means jail time." I kept my voice steady, not wanting to trigger her any more than she already was. "You need to end this, Anita. Stop with all these antics. Nobody else needs to get hurt."

"She's right, Anita," Weston called from behind me. "There's no need to draw this out anymore."

I could tell by his voice that he'd moved closer. But I still wasn't sure how to get out of the situation in one piece—unless I was able to literally talk Anita down from the ledge. That didn't seem like something I'd be able to do.

"I don't want to spend the rest of my days in jail." Her voice trembled, but her eyes still contained a distant, far-off look that signaled something wasn't quite right. "I'd rather die."

"Let Camryn go," Weston said. "She didn't do anything to deserve this."

Weston could talk a lot of people into a lot of things. But what about now? Would his charm work when everything was on the line?

"She should have left things alone." Anita lurched closer as if she might be about to tackle me.

I scooted back, nearly tumbling into Weston. He caught my elbows and pushed me back to my feet. Just as quickly, one of his arms went to my waist. He backed me farther down the catwalk as Anita crept closer.

"You might as well give it up," Anita hissed. "This won't end well for you."

"You sent me the note, didn't you?" I asked her, still hoping to talk my way out of this. "Ransacked the apartment? Ran me off the road?"

"I tried everything to keep you quiet. You didn't take the hint."

"Are you the one who stole my purse also?" I asked.

"I heard you'd taken a video, and I got nervous." She shrugged. "I gave you plenty of chances to back off. Whatever happens now, it's your fault!"

"Anita . . ." Weston's voice trailed. "You have the power to change the outcome of this situation."

Anita swiped her knife in a wide arc.

I was far enough away that it didn't touch me, but I heard the blade slicing through the air.

Weston gripped my arm and tugged me away from Anita. We scooted around the corner but were still a long way away from getting to the ladder that led down to safety.

We had to go across the stage area first.

That presented a lot of opportunities for things to go wrong. Too many opportunities.

My head swam again at the thought.

Was there any worse place I could have picked to confront Anita? It didn't appear that was the case.

I stared at Anita, wishing I could reach through to her and make her listen. "The students trusted you. How could you turn on them like this? How could you have exploited Heather's peanut allergy like that?"

"I would do anything for my daughter. Anything."

It made me think back to my conversation with Skittles, about how love looked like a multitude of emotions sometimes. In this case, the emotion was definitely misplaced.

"Stop walking!" Anita shouted. "If you don't stop right now, I'm going to run at you and not stop until this knife is in your chest. I don't have anything to lose anymore. You've ruined everything!"

Judging by the look on Anita's face, she was serious.

Weston and I needed to make a choice, and we need to make it fast.

***

"CAM, RUN!" Weston pushed me behind him.

I knew what he was doing. He was going to take that knife for me.

But I couldn't let him do that. I was the one who had gotten us into the situation.

I looked up in time to see Anita charging forward, just as she'd threatened.

"No!" I yelled.

I held my breath, unable to breathe as I waited for what would happen next.

I glanced at Weston, wondering if I could pull him out of the way. Wondering if there was something else I could do.

But, based on the crazy look in Anita's eyes, nothing was going to stop her. Nothing.

"Dear God . . ." The prayer slipped from my lips.

I tugged Weston back, trying to buy more time.

But I knew he was only seconds from death or serious injury.

Just as Anita let out a grunt, a new noise filled the air.

Gunfire.

I held my breath again as I waited to see what exactly was happening.

I grabbed Weston's bicep, waiting to hear him yell with pain.

Instead, Anita's face morphed from determined to alarmed.

The knife dropped from her hand and slipped to the stage below.

Then Anita fell onto the catwalk. Blood bloomed on the back of her shirt.

Someone from below had shot her.

I glanced beneath me, and I saw Detective Garrison standing there, gun raised.

His bullet had hit its mark.

Weston turned around and looked at me. "Are you okay?"

I nodded, still feeling numb and in shock. "Thanks to you."

He turned back to Anita and put a finger to her neck. "She still has a pulse."

"Clear the way! Paramedics need to come up!" someone yelled from below.

Weston started to move when I heard Anita speak again.

"Tell my daughter I love her."

My heart pounded in my chest. "I will. I will. I promise."

Before I could say anything else, Weston took my arm. We hurried toward the ladder and climbed down. As soon as we hit the floor, paramedics rushed up. I wasn't sure how they were going to get Anita down, but they'd figure it out.

Weston glanced at me, and our gazes locked. The next instant, he pulled me into a hug.

As I felt my knees go weak, I let him hold me. It was nice to have somebody else hold me up.

CHAPTER THIRTY-SIX

"THAT WAS A CLOSE ONE." Detective Garrison paused backstage as officers swarmed the area. "Good job calling me. As soon as I got your message, I headed toward the school."

I glanced at Weston. "In my defense, I tried to call you too. Your phone must have been on silent mode."

He rubbed his jaw. "Sorry about that. Thankfully, Langston told me what you were doing. You could have died up there."

His words instantly sobered me. If I'd died, Scarlett would have lost both of her parents. I couldn't let that happen to her. At least, not as much as I could control. I shouldn't have taken the risk I did tonight, but, thankfully, everything had ended up okay.

Next time I might not be as lucky.

"I just didn't want the killer to get away," I finally said. "I wanted to catch her in the act."

A mixture of disapproval and admiration filled Garrison's gaze. "And that's exactly what you did. I suppose maybe I should tell you good job."

"And I should tell you good job as well. I'm sure this is going to look good on your record."

The two of us exchanged a smile.

"By the way, I just heard that Anita is at the hospital, and she's stable," Garrison said. "She has a long road ahead of her—a road that will mostly contain jail time."

"It's just sad that she felt like she had to go to such an extreme to get what she wanted." I shook my head. "But I'm glad this is all over now."

Just then, Joseph rushed up the steps at the front of the stage and joined the three of us near the podium. "Camryn. Weston. I'm so glad the two of you are okay."

As usual, he was sweating like a soldier under fire.

I wondered if Anita had made up everything about him regretting hiring me. I didn't know, and I didn't plan on asking. The fact was, Joseph would do anything to protect the school's legacy.

I didn't think he would go as far as to kill someone because that would be creating a whole different kind of legacy—but he was desperate to preserve the school's image. I needed to remind myself to be more guarded around him, just in case.

"So are we." Weston cast me a knowing smile.

"Now that this . . . issue . . . has been resolved, does that mean you'll soon be leaving here?" Garrison asked.

I glanced at Joseph, watching for his reaction.

His expression remained unchanged.

"We would be honored if you'd stay around for a bit longer, Camryn," he finally said. "It's going to take a while for our image to recover, and we could use someone like you on our team for a little longer."

I was glad he said that because I wasn't ready to leave this place yet. I felt like I still needed more resolution. "I'd be more than happy to stay."

Joseph smiled. "I'm pleased to hear that. Thank you for all your help with this. Maybe we can finally put this behind us."

"That's what I'm hoping as well. I also want to talk to you about starting a program for kids who aren't accepted into school here. Maybe some type of bridge program that will help them grow their skills until they can audition again . . ."

"I think that sounds like a great idea," Weston said. "That way, it's not all-in or all-out. But there's an in-between."

Joseph glanced around before casting a nervous smile. "We'll bring it up at the next board meeting."

As he wandered over to talk to some of the school's trustees, I turned back to Weston. "It looks like you're going to have to work with me for a little while longer."

"I think I can handle that."

I grinned. "I'm happy to hear that. I really mean that. Thank you for everything that you've done for me. I probably wouldn't be alive right now if it weren't for you."

"Anything for you, Cam. Anything."

Maybe I'd come back here just for closure—closure with Weston.

Or maybe it was for some other reason.

I was going to stick around longer to find out . . . but I hoped that solving murders wouldn't be added to my résumé.

If you enjoyed this book, please consider leaving a review!

USA TODAY BESTSELLING AUTHOR
CHRISTY BARRITT
SCHOOL OF HARD ROCKS
BOOK TWO
CRIME STRIKES A CHORD

ALSO BY CHRISTY BARRITT:

YOU MIGHT ALSO ENJOY ...
THE SQUEAKY CLEAN MYSTERY SERIES

On her way to completing a degree in forensic science, Gabby St. Claire drops out of school and starts her own crime-scene cleaning business. When a routine cleaning job uncovers a murder weapon the police overlooked, she realizes that the wrong person is in jail. She also realizes that crime scene cleaning might be the perfect career for utilizing her investigative skills.

#1 Hazardous Duty

#2 Suspicious Minds

#2.5 It Came Upon a Midnight Crime (novella)

#3 Organized Grime

#4 Dirty Deeds

#5 The Scum of All Fears

THE WORST DETECTIVE EVER:

I'm not really a private detective. I just play one on TV.

Joey Darling, better known to the world as Raven Remington, detective extraordinaire, is trying to separate herself from her invincible alter ego. She played the spunky character for five years on the hit TV show *Relentless*, which catapulted her to fame and into the role of Hollywood's sweetheart. When her marriage falls apart, her finances dwindle to nothing, and her father disappears, Joey finds herself on the Outer Banks of North Carolina, trying to piece together her life away from the limelight. But as people continually mistake her for the character she played on TV, she's tasked with solving real life crimes . . . even though she's terrible at it.

ABOUT THE AUTHOR

USA Today has called Christy Barritt's books "scary, funny, passionate, and quirky."

Christy writes both mystery and romantic suspense novels that are clean with underlying messages of faith. Her books have won the Daphne du Maurier Award for Excellence in Suspense and Mystery, have been twice nominated for the Romantic Times Reviewers' Choice Award, and have finaled for both a Carol Award and Foreword Magazine's Book of the Year.

She is married to her Prince Charming, a man who thinks she's hilarious—but only when she's not trying to be. Christy is a self-proclaimed klutz, an avid music lover who's known for spontaneously bursting into song, and a road trip aficionado.

When she's not working or spending time with her family, she enjoys singing, playing the guitar, and exploring small, unsuspecting towns where people have no idea how accident-prone she is.

Find Christy online at:
    www.christybarritt.com
    www.facebook.com/christybarritt
    www.twitter.com/cbarritt

Sign up for Christy's newsletter to get information on all of her latest releases here: **www.christybarritt.com/newsletter-sign-up/**

If you enjoyed this book, please consider leaving a review.

www.ingramcontent.com/pod-product-compliance
Lightning Source LLC
Chambersburg PA
CBHW031959150726

47990CB00005B/1772

9798869260253